ARE
WE
THERE
YET?

Also by David Levithan

Boy Meets Boy

ARE
WE
THERE
YET?

DAVID LEVITHAN

HarperCollins*Publishers*

First published in the USA by Alfred A. Knopf 2005
First published in Great Britain in 2007 by HarperCollins*Publishers* Ltd
77-85 Fulham Palace Road, Hammersmith, London, W6 8JB
This edition published 2013

The HarperCollins website address is: www.harpercollins.co.uk

2

Copyright © David Levithan 2005

David Levithan asserts the moral right to be identified
as the author of this work.

ISBN 978-0-00-753304-6

Printed and bound in England by
Clays Ltd, St Ives plc

To Mom, Dad and Adam
(here, there and everywhere)

ACKNOWLEDGMENTS

Thanks to my wonderful parents and my wonderful brother for their support far and wide. Thanks to my friends and family, who have been my faithful travelling companions, whether flying across an ocean or simply strolling through the streets of Soho. I love the moments we share.

Thank you specifically to the friends who have helped me with this book, in its valentine-story incarnation or on the road to its present form: Karen Popernik, Dan Poblocki and Jack Lienke. Thank you also to the new friends I've found so far in my life as an author – librarians and teachers and readers and fellow writers and editors who've taken me and my writing to such incredible places. It means the world to me.

Thank you to everyone at Knopf for giving my books such a remarkable home. Thank you in particular to Melissa Nelson for her exquisite design (as always).

Thank you to the Simko Family Collection (curated by Patti Ann, John and Zach) for the loan of their Italian Sno-globes.

Be we in Paris or in Lansing, my editor, Nancy Hinkel, is entrancing. There's no one I'd rather dance among the chandeliers with.

Finally, thank you to Jen and Paolo for showing me all of the things – especially love – that can be found in translation. As I write this, Alessandro is five days old. May he journey both close and far to discover the world.

DEPARTURE

THE PHONE RINGS AT AN UNGODLY HOUR. ELIJAH LOOKS AT THE BLUR of his clock as he reaches for the sound. Eleven in the morning on a Saturday. Who can be calling him at eleven in the morning on a Saturday? Cal, his best friend, stirs from somewhere on the floor. Elijah picks up the phone and murmurs a greeting.

"Oh goodness, did I wake you?" Elijah's mother asks, her voice so much louder than the dream he'd been having.

"No, no," he says, disguising his own voice to sound awake. "Not at all."

"Good, because I have some great news for you..."

His mother is talking about Italy and Elijah's brother Danny and luxury accommodations. He thinks his brother has won a prize on a game show or something. Cal starts hitting his sneaker like it's a snooze button. He tells her to go back to sleep.

"What did you say?" his mother asks. "Will you go?"

"Does Danny want me to go?"

Elijah doubts highly that Danny wants him to go.

"Of course he does."

Elijah still doubts that Danny wants him to go.

Cal is awake now, rubbing her eyes. Elijah's boarding school

9

frowns on having overnight guests, but Elijah doesn't really care if it frowns.

Elijah covers the receiver and whispers to Cal, "It's my mom. I think she wants to know if I want to go to Italy with my brother."

Cal shrugs, then nods.

That's enough for Elijah.

"Sure, Mom," he says. "And thanks."

ELIJAH ALWAYS SAYS THANK YOU, AND OFTENTIMES SAYS PLEASE.

"You're such a relic," Cal will taunt him playfully.

"Thank you," Elijah will reply.

Elijah learned quickly that saying thank you garners a variety of reactions. Some people (like his brother) can't handle it. Other people (like Cal) are amused. Most people are impressed, whether consciously or not. He'll be offered the last slice of pizza, or the last hit from the bong.

"You're a relic, not a saint," Cal will continue, dragging him to the next party, parties called *gatherings*, dances called *raves*. Where she leads, he will follow. She tousles his blond-brown hair and buys him blue sunglasses. He playfully disapproves of her random boyfriends and girlfriends, and gives her flowers for no reason. They smoke pot, but not cigarettes. At the end of most parties, they can be found woozily collecting cans and bottles for the recycling bin.

Elijah had planned to spend the summer hanging out with Cal and their other friends in Providence. At first, his parents weren't too thrilled about the idea. ("Hang out?" his mother said. "Sweetheart, *laundry* hangs out.") Now he's being sent to Italy for nine days.

"I'm going to miss you," Cal says a few nights before Elijah is scheduled to leave. They are walking home from a midnight movie at the Avon. The June night is warm and cool, as only June nights can be. The air is scored by the faint whir of cars passing elsewhere. Elijah inhales deeply and takes hold of Cal's hand. Her hair – dyed raven black – flutters despite itself.

"I love it here," Elijah says. He is not afraid to say it. "I love it here, this moment, everything." He stops looking at the sky and turns to Cal.

"Thank you," he whispers.

Cal holds his hand tighter. They walk together in silence. When they get back to school, they find four of their friends on the common room's lime-green couch. Mindy, Ivan, Laurie and Sue are playing spin the bottle – just to be playful, just to be kissed. The moment shifts; Elijah is still happy, but it's a different happiness. A daylight happiness, a lightbulb happiness. Cal arches her eyebrow, Elijah laughs, and together they join the game.

Elijah is the first to grow unconquerably tired, the first to call it a night. Cal is still laughing, changing the CD, flirting with the lava lamp. Elijah says his goodnights and is given goodnights in return. The world already misfocusing. He makes his way to bed.

Ten minutes later, there are two knocks from the hallway. The door opens and Cal appears, brightness behind her. It is time for their ritual, their nightly ritual, which Elijah thought Cal had forgotten. Sometimes she does, and that's OK. But tonight she is in the room. Elijah moves over in his bed and Cal lies down beside him.

"Do you wonder...?" she begins. This is their game – *Do you wonder?* Every night – every night when it's possible – the last thing to be heard is the asking without answer. They stare at the glow-in-the-dark planets on the ceiling, or turn sideways to trace each other's blue-black outlines, trying to detect the shimmer of silver as they speak.

This night, Cal asks, "Do you wonder if we'll ever learn to sleep with our eyes open?"

And in return, Elijah asks, "Do you think there can be such a thing as too much happiness?"

This is Elijah's favourite time. He rarely knows what he is going to say, and then suddenly it's there. Above them. Lifting.

A few minutes pass. Cal sits up and puts her hand on Elijah's shoulder.

"Goodnight, sleep tight," she whispers.

"Don't let the bedbugs bite," he chimes, nestling deeper under the covers.

Cal smiles and returns to the party. Elijah rearranges his pillows and fits himself within the sheets. And as he does, he wonders. He wonders about goldfish asleep with their eyes open. He wonders about Italy, about his parents, about whether the stars will be brighter in Venice. He hears voices at a distance, the lively sound of voices from the common room. Like the spots of colour whenever he closes his eyes. He closes his eyes. He thinks about what a wonderful friend Cal is. How lucky he is to have such friends, all of his friends. He is happy. He is almost empty with happiness...

As Elijah "hangs out" for the summer, as he smokes and dopes and lazes and does who knows what else (according to his brother), Danny toils and roils away at Gladner, Gladner, Smith & Jones. The two senior Gladners (of no relation – they sat next to each other at Harvard Business School) have taken Danny under their wingtips. Their secretary saves him a seat in the boardroom and provides him with an ample supply of Mark Cross pens. He walks the halls with a boy-wonder halo, the recipient of enough gratitude to deflect all but the pettiest begrudgements. He is twenty-three years old.

People at work pay attention to Danny Silver because he single-thoughtedly saved the Miss Jane's Homemade Petite Snack Cakes account (Gladner, Gladner's largest). Danny specialises in crisis control, and the crisis faced by Miss Jane's was a doozy: a bored and crusading *Washington Post* reporter discovered that the neon-pink frosting on Miss Jane's most popular snack cake ("the Divine") was made with the same ingredients as the nation's bestselling lipstick ("Pink Nightshade"). Consumers were not pleased. Miss Jane's stock plummeted; the company's profits seemed poised to go the way of a dung-coated Twinkie.

Enter Danny Silver. (Imagine this to be a grand entrance – the boardroom door opens, Miss Jane's directors all turn in unison to see their fair-haired saviour. In truth, Danny Silver first appeared to the cupcake conspirators via e-mail, and his hair isn't fair. But the effect was the same.) While others advised refusal and rebuttal, Danny suggested humility and humour. A press conference was announced, during which the company president expressed shock and dismay, and pledged an overhaul of the Divine, wherein the frosting would be made from purely organic sources. He also made clear that the rest of the snack cakes in the Miss Jane's family were "one hundred per cent cosmetic-free." As soon as Danny heard the reporters laugh with this, he knew everything would be OK.

But OK wasn't good enough. The company had to emerge triumphant.

In a mere thirty-nine hours, Danny had come up with his masterstroke. It came to him as he paced his Upper East Side apartment, throwing clothes into the hamper, figuring out which kind of pasta to boil for dinner. (He loves to tell this story; it's one of his best stories.) As Danny paced, he thought of cakes, cream fillings, cafeterias and childhood. The idea appeared. It wove itself brilliantly within him. He did not hesitate. He called Jones, who called Smith, who paged Gladner, who woke up Gladner at his girlfriend's apartment in the Village. Three hours later, the bigwigs gathered – a war room – as Danny bounced among them. A conference call was placed to "Miss Jane" (aka

Arthur Swindland, 61, renowned throughout the world for his collection of celebrity polo sticks).

A scant two weeks later, America and Europe witnessed Miss Jane's First Annual Bake Sale. (The rest of the world would continue to eat lipstick frosting.) Miss Jane's employees and certain grandmothers-for-hire set up tables in supermarkets across the land, all selling snack cakes. The profits would go to the newly formed Miss Jane's Homemade Petite Snack Cake Centre for World Peace. Katie Couric herself bought a snack cake on live television. Oprah invited Miss Jane to be her guest on a programme stressing "corporate responsibility in the kinder, gentler age." (When Mrs Silver saw this show, she knew her son had arrived. Making corporate billions was one thing – but to be on *Oprah*! was true accomplishment. Elijah didn't bother to watch.) Miss Jane (née Mr Swindland) was so impressed with Danny that he earmarked .01% of the MJHPSCCWP's profits to the charity of Danny's choice. (The rest would be distributed to Shriners organizations around the world.)

As his star rises, Danny finds himself working longer and longer hours. By the time he leaves the office, the wastebaskets have been emptied and the floors have been vacuumed. He has begun to forget what his apartment looks like. (His friends might say the same about him.) Gladner and Gladner (both devotees of Ted Newness, the management guru) tell Danny they will give him a raise – as long as he takes a vacation in the month of July.

Three days later, Mrs Silver calls with her offer.

Danny Silver doesn't doubt for a second that he's being tricked into taking a trip to Italy.

"It's all *prepaid*," his mother proclaims. "I know this is such short notice. But I just don't think that your father can go. Italy isn't a place for sitting. And his leg – well, you know your father's leg. We had hoped it would be OK by now. But who can know such things?"

Danny's father is fine. The day before, he played eighteen holes of golf.

"How are you feeling, Pop?" Danny asks once his mother has passed over the phone.

"Oh, I don't know. The leg's been acting up."

"But you were playing golf yesterday."

"Yes, yes, yes. I must have overextended myself. A damn shame. About Italy, I mean. But Mom tells me you and Elijah are going to go..."

Aha, Danny thinks. *The hitch.*

There is a whisper and a shuffling noise as Mrs Silver takes back the phone.

"I know, I know," Danny's mom says as her husband recedes to the couch. "I hadn't mentioned that part. But it's only fair. We have two tickets. Two sons. And it's prepaid. Nonrefundable. Your father can't go. So I can't go."

"Ask the Himmelfarbs," Danny offers. "They're your best friends, after all."

"The *Himmelfarbs*? Do you know how much this trip costs?"

18

Mrs Silver takes a deep breath. "No. You and Elijah should take the tickets. It's a week. Nine days."

Nine days with Elijah. Nine days with Quiet Boy, Mr Virtue, Boy Misunderstood. Elijah, who never seemed to change. Not since he was ten or so and started to grow quiet. His mind seems to be working on two levels at once – *pass the salt* and *contemplate the pureness of the clouds*. He is always dazed, and he is always kind. Faultlessly kind.

Danny can't stand it.

"Have you asked Elijah how he feels about this?" Danny is hoping that Elijah might still say no. Since Elijah is still in high school and Danny is in the Working World, the two of them rarely have to see each other.

"Yes," his mother replies. "He thinks it's a great idea."

Danny can hear his father chuckle in the background. He can imagine his father giving his mother a thumbs-up sign and his mother smiling. *Prepaid. No refunds.*

His mother continues. "It's over the week of July Fourth. You'd only have to take six days off from work. And you haven't been *anywhere* this year."

"OK, OK, OK," Danny relents. He wonders if it counts as being tricked if he knows what's really going on.

"You'll go?"

Danny smiles. "There is nothing in the world I would rather do."

There is still a chance that Elijah will back out...

BUT NO.

At one in the morning the night before departure, Danny wakes up with a start.

He hasn't talked to Elijah since their mother made the offer. He should have talked to him, and has tried to, but whenever he's called, someone else has answered. Probably some pothead incapable of taking a message. Danny wants to be well-Fodored and well-Frommered by the time he sets down on Italian soil. But what will Elijah want to do? What does Elijah *normally* do?

I'll have to talk to him. For a week. Nine days.

But about what?

How's life? (Two-minute answer.) *How's school?* (Five minutes, tops.) *How's life with the dope fiends?* (Maybe not a minute – maybe just a Look.) *What do you want to do today?* (That one could stretch out – maybe twenty minutes each day, depending on the repetition of shrugs.) *So isn't this a fine mess we're in?* (Rhetorical – no help.)

Danny gets out of bed, switches on the light and squints. He counts his traveller's checks; he's bringing extra spending money, assuming Elijah won't have any. He takes out the list of gifts he has to buy, makes sure it's in his wallet, and makes sure his wallet is on the bureau by the keys.

He knows he is missing something. He is always missing something. He can never get past the first step of finding it, which is knowing what it is.

He stays up most of the night, doing things like this. He doesn't want to forget anything. And, more than that, he wants to think of something to say.

Seven years apart. Danny can remember the moment his father called to say Elijah had been born. Elijah can't picture Danny younger than ten, except from the photographs that hung around the house long after Danny left for college.

They never had to share a room, except when they went down to the shore. Spending the day by the pool, broken by stretches of playing on the beach. Danny was the Master Builder of sandcastles, Elijah his ready First Assistant. No two castles were the same, and in that way no two days were ever the same. One day would bring the Empire State Building, the next a dragon. Danny always sketched it first on the surface of the beach. Then Elijah dug, providing sand and more sand and more and more sand until he hit the water beneath and had to move a little bit over to start again. As Danny created windows out of Popsicle sticks and towers out of turned-over buckets, Elijah would wander wide to collect shells. Sometimes the shells would be decoration and other times they would become the residents of the castle. Extended shell families, each with a name and a story. As Danny dipped his hand in water to pat the walls smooth, Elijah would explain what went on inside, making the shape and the hour more real than Danny could have ever made alone.

There would always be extra shells, and at night Elijah would line them up on the dresser, sometimes according to size, sometimes according to colour. Then he would crawl into his bed and Danny would crawl only two feet away into his own bed. From there, Danny would read Elijah a story. Whatever older-kid books Danny was reading – Narnia being chronicled, time being wrinkled – he would send through the stillness to his brother. This was supposed to put Elijah to sleep, but it never did. He always wanted to find out where his brother would take him next.

CAL DRIVES ELIJAH DOWN FROM PROVIDENCE IN HER BITCHIN' CAMARO. It was buck-naked white until she and Elijah covered it with the primary-colour handprints of all their friends. It's a 1979 model, the transmission is crap, and it goes from 0 to 60 in just under four minutes. But, man, once it gets to 60! The Camaro is, joyously, a convertible. Cal and Elijah zoom down I-95, blasting pop from the year of the car's birth, swerving from lane to lane. When they can hear each other over the wind and the music, they speak Connecticut: I *will not Stamford this type of behaviour. What's Groton into you? What did Danbury his Hartford? New Haven can wait. Darien't no place I'd rather be.*

As they reach the New York state line, Elijah feels the urge to turn back. He can't pinpoint why. It seems the wrong time to be leaving. He doesn't want to step out of the present, this present. Because once he does, there will be college applications and college acceptances (just one will do) and the last of everything (last class, last party, last night, last day, last goodbye), and then the world will change forever and he will go to college and eventually become an adult. That is not what he wants. He does not want those complications, that change. Not now.

He tells himself to get a grip. Cal is driving him forward. Cal and everyone else will be here when he returns. It's like he's travelling into another dimension. Time here will stop. Because he is entering Family Standard Time. None of it will carry over to Cal, to the Camaro, to the state of Connecticut.

He will go with his brother. He will have a good time. Life will be waiting for him when he gets back. Not a bad deal.

Elijah smiles at Cal. But Cal isn't looking. Then she turns to him as if she knows. She smiles back and blasts the music louder.

Dᴀɴɴʏ's ᴍᴏᴛʜᴇʀ ᴅʀɪᴠᴇs ʜɪᴍ. Hᴇ ʟɪᴠᴇs ɪɴ Nᴇᴡ Yᴏʀᴋ Cɪᴛʏ. Therefore, he doesn't have a car of his own. When he wants to travel far, he signs out a company car. But this time, his mother won't hear of it. Those are her exact words – "I won't hear of it" – as if it's news of an ignoble death.

"Just be nice to him," his mother is saying now. He's heard this before. *Just be nice to him*. He heard it after he dared Elijah to poke the hanger in the socket. After he put glue in Elijah's socks, telling him it was foot lotion. After he turned off the hot water while Elijah was in the shower. For the fifth time.

Elijah could have retaliated. But he never even tattled. Elijah has always taken his mother's words to heart. Elijah can just be nice. Sometimes, Danny thinks this is all Elijah can be.

"I *mean it*," his mother stresses. Then her tone shifts and Danny thinks, *Yes, she does mean it*.

"I worry about you." She looks straight ahead while turning the radio down. Danny thinks it remarkable that she still doesn't look old. "Really, I do worry about you. I worry about you both, and that you won't have each other. There aren't many times that I wish you were younger. But when I

26

remember the way the two of you would get along – you cared about him *so much*. When he was a baby, you were always feeling his head and coming to me and saying he had a fever. Or you'd wake us up, worrying he'd been kidnapped. All night, I had to reassure you that he was OK. Staying up with the older son instead of the baby. But it was worth it. In the middle of the night, when you couldn't sleep, you'd beg me to take you to Eli's room. And when I did, you would sing to him. He was already asleep, and still you wanted to sing him a lullaby. I would whisper with you. It was so wonderful, even if it was three in the morning. For a few years after, you watched over him. And then something happened. And I wish I knew what it was. Because I'd undo it in a second."

"But, Mom—"

"Don't interrupt." She holds up her hand. "You know it's important to your father. It's important to me. It's also important to *you*. I don't think you realise it yet. You both can be so nice and so smart and so generous. I just don't understand why you can't be that way with each other."

Danny wants to say something to assure his mother. He wants to tell her he loves Elijah, but he's afraid it won't sound convincing.

So they remain silent. Eventually, Danny turns the radio up a little and Mrs Silver shifts lanes to make the airport turnoff. She asks Danny if he's remembered his traveller's checks, his passport, his guidebooks.

"Of course I remembered them," Danny responds. "I'm your son, after all."

That gets a smile. And Danny is happy, because even if he can't do anything else right, at least he can still make his mother smile.

Cal doesn't want to stay for the Silver family reunion. After she speeds away in the bitchin' Camaro, Elijah waves goodbye for a full minute before entering the airport.

He finds his mother and brother easily enough.

"So where's your girlfriend?" Danny asks as Mrs Silver hugs Elijah tightly.

"She's not my girlfriend."

"So where is she?" Danny is wearing a suit. For the airplane.

"She had to go." Elijah can't stand still. His sneakers keep squeaking on the linoleum. He doesn't know whether it's the suit that makes Danny look old or whether it's just life. He is *filling out*, as their mother would say, as if the outline of his adult self was always there, waiting. Elijah thinks this is scary.

"I brought you danish," Mrs Silver says, handing Elijah a white box tied with bakery string.

"You're the greatest," Elijah announces. And he means it. Because he knows the bakery, he can see his mother holding the number in her hand, hoping against hope that they'll have blueberry, because that's his favourite.

Mrs Silver blushes. Danny gazes intently at a newsstand.

"I need to buy gum," he says.

"Oh, I have gum." Mrs Silver's purse is opened in a flash.

"Yeah, *sugarless*. I don't want sugarless. I'll just go get some Juicy Fruit, OK?"

"Oh," Mrs Silver sighs. "Do you need money?"

Danny smiles. "I think I can afford a pack of gum, Mom." Then he's off, dropping his bag at Elijah's feet.

"I'll take some Trident," Elijah offers.

Mrs Silver rummages again and unearths a blue pack and a green pack.

"Sorry, no red," she says with a smile as she hands the gum over.

"No problem. Thanks." Elijah tucks the gum into his pocket. He doesn't like either blue or green, but he doesn't mind taking it. Someone else on the plane might want some.

While Danny buys his gum (and newspapers and Advil and a hardcover legal thriller), Elijah asks about his father's leg, and she tells him it's getting better. He thanks her again for the trip — he is *sure* it's going to be great, there are *so many* things he wants to see. She thinks his hair is a little too long, but doesn't say anything. (The telltale look at his collar gives her away.)

"So are we ready?" Danny is back.

"Ready as we'll never be," Elijah replies. Danny's tie is caught in his shoulder-bag strap. Elijah is inordinately pleased by this.

THERE'S AN ISSUE THAT HAS TO BE RESOLVED IMMEDIATELY. DANNY, bearer of the tickets, brings it up as soon as he and Elijah are through security.

"So," he asks, "do you want the window seat or the middle seat?"

"Up to you."

Of course. Danny knew this was going to happen. Clearly, the window seat is preferable to the middle seat. And politeness decrees that whoever chooses first will have to choose the middle seat. Elijah *must* know this. Typical Elijah. He seems so kind. But really, he is passive-aggressive.

(*"Why can't you be more like your brother?"* his parents would ask when he was seventeen.

"Because he's ten!" Danny would shout before slamming his door closed.)

"You don't have any preference?" Danny asks. "None whatsoever?"

Elijah shrugs. "Whatever you want. I'm just going to sleep."

"But wouldn't it be easier for you to have the window seat, then?" Danny continues, a little too urgently.

31

"It's no big deal. I'll take the middle seat if you want me to."

Great. Now Elijah is the martyr. Danny can't stand it when Elijah plays the martyr. But if it gets him the window seat...

"Fine. You can have the middle seat."

"Thanks."

At the gate they have to cool their heels for almost an hour. Danny is bothered despite his desire not to be bothered. (It bothers him even more to be bothered against his will.) Elijah reads a British music magazine and listens to his headphones. Because Elijah slumps in his seat, Danny doesn't realise they're now the same height. All he notices is Elijah's ragged haircut, the small silver hoop piercing the top of his earlobe.

Danny tries to read the book he bought, but it doesn't work. He is too distracted. Not only because he's bothered. He is slowly crossing over. He is realising for the first time that, yes, he is about to go to Italy. Every trip has this time – the shift into happening. Before things can go badly or go well, there is always the first moment when expectation turns to *now*.

Danny relaxes a little. He puts away his book and takes out his *Fodor's Venice*. Minutes later, there is a call for boarding. Danny gathers his things for pre-boarding. Elijah pointedly makes them wait until their row is called.

"You're sure you don't want the window seat?" Danny asks as they walk the ramp to the plane.

"Not unless you want the middle seat," Elijah answers.

Danny waves the subject away.

Elijah charms the flight crew from the get-go. He asks the flight attendants how they are doing. He looks at the cockpit with such awe that the pilot smiles. Danny manoeuvres Elijah to their seats, then has to get up again to find overhead compartment space (the rest of the row illegally pre-boarded).

Once they settle into their seats, Danny expects Elijah to strike up a conversation with his aisle-seat neighbour. But Elijah keeps a respectful distance. He says hello. He tells his neighbour to let him know if his music gets too loud. And then he puts on his headphones, even though he's supposed to wait.

Danny offers Elijah a guidebook. Elijah says he'll look at it later. Danny doesn't want Elijah to wait until the last minute (so predictable), but doesn't bother to say anything. He just sits back and prepares for the flight. He is ready for takeoff. He loves takeoff. Takeoff is precisely the thing he wants his life to be.

As the plane lifts, Danny sees that his brother's teeth are clenched. Elijah's fingers grip at his shirt, twisting it.

"Are you OK?" Danny asks as the plane bumps a little.

Elijah opens his eyes.

"I'm fine," he says, his face deathly pale.

Then he shuts his eyes again and makes his music louder.

Danny stares at his brother for a moment, then closes his own eyes. *Fodor's* can wait for a few minutes. Right now, all Danny wants to do is rise.

Eᴌɪᴊᴀʜ ᴛʀɪᴇꜱ ᴛᴏ ᴛʀᴀɴꜱʟᴀᴛᴇ ᴛʜᴇ ᴍᴜꜱɪᴄ ɪɴᴛᴏ ᴘɪᴄᴛᴜʀᴇꜱ. Hᴇ ᴛʀɪᴇꜱ ᴛᴏ translate the music into thoughts. The plane is rising. Elijah is falling. He is seeing himself falling. He is blasting his music and still thinking that the whole *concept* of flying in an airplane is ridiculous. Like riding an aluminium toilet paper roll into outer space. What was he thinking? The music isn't translating. New Order cannot give him order. The bizarre love triangle is falling falling falling into the Bermuda Triangle.

Enough. This will have to be enough. The takeoff is almost over. The plane is flying steadily. Elijah inhales. He feels like he's gone an hour without breathing. Danny hasn't noticed. Danny is in Guidebook Country. Danny doesn't think twice about flying. He doesn't think twice about Elijah, really.

And if the plane were to crash... Elijah thinks about those final seconds. It could be as long as a minute, he's heard. What would he and Danny have to say to each other? Would everything suddenly be all right? Elijah thinks it might be, and that gives him a strange, momentary hope. Really, Cal would be a better doomsday companion. But Danny might do.

Imagining this scenario makes it OK. Elijah is OK as long as he can picture the wreck.

The captain turns off the fasten-seat-belt light. Danny unfastens his, even though he doesn't have to get up. Elijah leaves his on.

There is a tap on his shoulder. Not Danny. The other side.

"Excuse me," the woman next to him is saying. He takes the headphones off his ears, to be polite.

"Oh," the woman says, "you didn't have to do that. I have nothing against New Order, but it was getting a little loud, and you said to let you know..." She trails off.

"You like New Order?" Elijah asks.

The conversation begins.

E‍LIJAH LOVES THE CONVERSATION. WHATEVER CONVERSATION. THE tentative first steps. The shyness. Wondering whether it's going to happen and where it will go. He hates surface talk. He wants to dive right through it. With anyone. Because anyone he talks to seems to have something worthwhile to say.

The first steps are always the most awkward; he can tell almost immediately whether the surface is water or ice. The dancing of the eyes – *Are we going to have this conversation or not*? The first words – the common ground. *And how have you found yourself here*? *Where are you going*? – two simple questions that can lead to days of words.

"You like New Order?" Elijah asks.

The woman laughs. "In college. I loved New Order, but I had a Joy Division boyfriend. I wanted to hang out, he wanted to hang himself. We were doomed from the start."

The conversation continues.

DANNY CAN'T HELP BUT OVERHEAR THEM. ELIJAH IS, AFTER ALL, sitting at his elbow, taking up the armrest. Chatting away with the woman about disco groups. Unbelievable. Talking about college and girlfriends and Elijah's prom. ("She disappeared after the second song, but that was OK...") Danny usually assumes that lonely people are the only ones who have conversations on airplanes. Now he is faced with a dilemma: is he wrong, or is Elijah lonely? To sidestep the issue entirely, Danny decides that Elijah is an exception. Elijah, as always, is being unusually kind. While he himself is not lonely, he doesn't mind talking to lonely people. He is the Mother Teresa of banter.

Danny silently waits for his introduction, the moment when Elijah gestures to him and says, "This is my brother." Danny plans to put his guidebook down, smile a hello (taking a good look at the woman, who's about ten years older than him, but still attractive), and then make a hasty retreat back to Inns & Hotels.

But the conversation never drifts his way. Instead, they are talking about Roman Holiday. Danny can't believe it when Elijah says how much he loves Audrey Hepburn. He can understand it, but he can't *believe* it, for it's an adoration that he himself shares.

Danny isn't used to having something in common with Elijah, however slight. Their last name is the rope that ties them together. And now there is also this tiny thread. Audrey Hepburn.

Danny thinks about this for a moment. (If Elijah were to look over, he would notice his brother hasn't turned the page in the past ten minutes.) As Elijah and this stranger discuss the ending of *Roman Holiday* and how it makes them feel (sad, happy), Danny wonders whether it's true that *everyone*, at heart, likes Audrey Hepburn. So the similarity isn't that strange at all. It's as commonplace as the desire to eat when hungry. It doesn't link the two brothers any more than that.

That is something Danny can believe.

"SO THIS IS YOUR BROTHER?" PENELOPE WHISPERS, POINTING OVER Elijah's shoulder. He doesn't know why she is whispering. Then he turns and sees that Danny has fallen asleep on his tray table, the edge of his shoulder spotlighted by the overhead lamp.

"Do you think he needs a pillow?" Elijah asks.

"No. He'll be all right."

Elijah reaches over the armrest and presses the lightbulb button. Then he turns back to Penelope and asks her if she has any brothers or sisters. She has three sisters, one of whom is getting married in a matter of months.

"She's older than me, thank God," Penelope says with a sigh. "I have to wear this hideous dress. I told her – I said, 'This dress is hideous.' Her dress is gorgeous, by the way. Bridesmaids only exist to make the brides look good. I don't care what anyone says. It's not an honour. It's a mockery.

"Her dress has a train. When I saw it, I just started to cry. Not because I'm not the one who's getting married. I can handle that. But to see my sister in a white satin train – it was like we were playing dress-up again. She'd always let my mother's dresses trail behind her. Of course, I'd jump on them and try to trip her up. And I was always the one who got in trouble for the footprints – it didn't matter that the bottom was also covered with dust. Anyway – seeing her at the fitting, it struck me that I can't jump on her dress any more. I can't pull it over her head and show her underwear to the congregation. I can't even tell her that it isn't hers, that she has to put it back in the closet before our mother comes home. No, it's hers. And it's *her*."

Penelope shakes her head.

BOYS NEVER DRESS UP AS GROOMS, ELIJAH THINKS. *THEY NEVER practise their own weddings like girls do*. But there are other kinds of pairs. He remembers Batman and Robin. Luke and Han. Frodo and Aragorn. Cowboy and Indian.

There was only a year or two for those games, before Danny started dressing up in a different way. This time, the character he was playing was the cooler version of himself, shopping at the mall for the perfect costume, trying to blend in and stand out at the same time. It was never explained to Elijah, and he wasn't old enough to figure it out. All he knew was that one day his brother stopped wanting to be a superhero, stopped wanting to save their backyard world. Elijah stopped dressing up then, too. He retreated to the realm of his room, to his drawings, to his stuffed animals.

It wasn't the same.

Sisters dress up to rehearse for what will really happen to them. But brothers, Elijah realises, are never rehearsing that way. They rehearse their own illusions, until reality takes a turn and they are asked to rehearse for other things. You go to school. You graduate. You sell snack cakes. You hang up your cape and put on a suit.

Danny wakes up into the strange timeless nighttime of air travel. The window shades are drawn. The flight attendants float down the aisle like guardian angels. The guidebook has fallen at his feet. A woman is talking.

"...And then, it was the strangest thing, I walk into the room and *there's Courtney Love*. Have I told you this? No? Good. So I can't believe it. Now, this is after she was the lead singer of – what was it called? – Hole. Don't think I'm *that* old. I'm not that old. So it's after Hole, and I walk into the room, and there she is. I can't believe it. So I walk over to her and offer her a joint. Real cool. I can tell that my boyfriend's real impressed at how smooth I am. And she says yes. But *neither of us has a match*. I'm fumbling around, pulling the rolling papers and the dope out of my pockets, and I can't find a light! So my boyfriend just leans over, Courtney looks up at him, and all smooth, he lights her up. I'm still there fumbling. She says thanks to him, offers him a puff, and when he's done he *doesn't even offer it to me*. Because now they're talking and *sharing* and it's like I'm not even there. I say his name, and he just gives me one of those side smiles. I can't believe it. Some other guys join the conversation and I'm out of the circle. And I'm sure Courtney has seen me. But does she say anything? No. Not a word. My boyfriend's treating her like the Pope and my head's all screwed up, so I just say real loud, 'Well, why don't you just kiss her ring!' Everyone stares at me. Like, it makes perfect sense to me, but I'm the only person in the room with the context. I have to get out of there. Right away. My boyfriend's staring at me like I just called his mother a whore. And everyone else thinks I'm insulting Her Highness Courtney Love. So I run out of the room. But I'm not looking where I'm going – I crash into this guy in the doorway – *and that's how I met Billy Corgan*."

It's the woman next to Elijah. Danny is paralysed by her talking.

"No way!" Elijah exhales in admiration.

"Uh-huh."

Danny tries to fall back to sleep. He can't believe they're still awake.

Penelope sleeps soundly on Elijah's shoulder. Which is to say, soundlessly. He doesn't mind, even though it makes his arm sore. *Pins and needles*, Elijah thinks, and then he figures that having an arm full of pins and needles would hurt a hell of a lot more than this.

Danny stirs on the other side of him, waking up and turning to Elijah, his eyes unaccustomed to the simulated day. He registers Penelope on Elijah's shoulder and smiles groggily. *It's not like that*, Elijah wants to tell his brother. But he doesn't want to wake Penelope up.

It's like comfort, Elijah figures. Being a comfort is itself pretty comforting. Having someone find a place on your shoulder and be able to rest. Not seeing her face, but picturing it from her breath. Like a baby sleeping. Feeling her breath so slightly on his arm. Breathing in time. Comfort.

The quiet times are the ones to hold on to. In the quiet times, Elijah can think of other quiet times. Staring at the ceiling with Cal. Driving home from a concert, the road silent, the music in his head. Sharing a smile – for a moment – with a beautiful stranger passing in a car.

Beside Elijah, Danny shifts in his seat and signals to the flight attendant for another Diet Coke.

Danny would never let a stranger sleep on his shoulder, Elijah thinks. *Danny would be afraid of the germs.*

He closes his eyes and tries to drift off.

Amazing. Danny thinks it's amazing to be moving so fast without feeling movement. To be sitting in an airplane, travelling as fast as he's ever travelled, and still it feels like he's in a car, steadier than a train, not even as fast as sliding down a slide. *How can this be?* Danny wonders. He wants to ask someone. But who can he ask? Elijah, even if he were awake? The girl on Elijah's shoulder? (Isn't she a little old for him?) The pilot? No one. There's no one to tell him how it can feel so slow to go so fast.

The phone is embedded above the fold-down tray. He could make a collect call from above the Atlantic Ocean. He could slip the corporate card into the proper slot and dial any area code around the world. He does it – slips in the card – just to see what the dials are like. Thinking, *Wouldn't it be funny to slip your credit card into the slot, ten thousand miles in the air, and find a rotary phone?* But no – just the usual buttons. He can pretend it's home. Just a local call.

He pauses before dialing. He pauses too long. He pauses long enough to realise that no one comes instantly to mind. He doesn't have anyone instant. He doesn't have anyone worth a twenty-dollar-a-minute call.

Quietly, Danny places the phone back in its receiver. He presses a little too hard, and the woman in front of him rustles in her sleep. Danny looks at Elijah. He looks at Elijah's eyelids and tries to tell whether he's awake. He used to do that all the time when they were kids. Elijah would be faking sleep – he didn't want to leave the car, he didn't want to go to school – and Danny would catch the small, betraying twitches. He would try to point them out to his mom, and Elijah would mysteriously pop out of sleep before Danny could finish his sentence. Their mom would shake her head, more annoyed with Danny's tattling than with Elijah's fakery. Or so it seemed to Danny. Back then, and still.

Now Danny concentrates – staring into his brother's closed eyes. Waiting for one eye to open, to see if anyone's looking. Waiting for a telltale giggle of breath, or the twitch of an itching finger. Instead, he observes Elijah and the woman both breathing to the same silent measure. Crescendo. Diminuendo. Rise. Fall. Speed and slowness.

DANNY REMEMBERS THE NIGHTMARES HE WOULD HAVE. THE STRANGERS climbing through the window and stealing Elijah from the crib. He remembers waking the house without waking the baby. Running to Elijah's room to make sure. Because if Elijah was OK, that meant everything was fine.

E<small>LIJAH TRAVELS IN AND OUT OF SLEEP, LIKE THE AIRPLANE TRAVELLING</small> in and out of clouds. Moments of fleeting wakefulness, dreamlike. The rituals of airline travel, meant to guard against your fears. Words of conversation. The echo of the in-flight movie from too-loud headphones many rows behind. The wheels of the beverage cart and the crisp opening of a soda can. The pad of feet in the aisle. A child's questions. The flipping of a magazine page. Penelope's breathing. The sound of speeding air. The realisation that clouds sound no different than air.

He dreams of Cal's Camaro and of driving to Italy.

Then he wakes up, and he is there.

VENICE

THE PLANE LANDS IMPECCABLY. DANNY IS UP AND ANGLING FOR THE aisle before the captain's announcement can tell him to keep his seat belt on. Elijah watches him with a certain degree of embarrassment. He can't see what the rush is. It's not like they can leave the plane any faster. All it means is they'll have their bags in their laps for that much longer. Even the flight attendants are still strapped in; they can't make Danny sit down. Along with the rest of the passengers, Elijah hopes a sudden stop will jolt Danny to the ground.

Elijah remains in his seat until the plane has come to a complete stop. Danny passes over their carry-ons. Penelope leans over and says she can't believe she's finally in Venice.

Elijah nods his head and looks out the window.

Venice.

But not really Venice. The airport.

It is raining outside.

Eʟɪᴊᴀʜ ᴄᴀɴ'ᴛ ʜᴇʟᴘ ɪᴛ. Hᴇ ꜱᴄᴀɴꜱ ᴛʜᴇ ᴄʀᴏᴡᴅ ᴀᴛ ᴛʜᴇ ɢᴀᴛᴇ ᴏᴜᴛꜱɪᴅᴇ of customs, looking to see if someone is waiting for him. As if Cal could truly drive the bitchin' Camaro across the Atlantic Ocean and wait with a lei, just to be inappropriate.

"Let's go," Danny says, hiking his bag higher on his shoulder. "And tie your shoelaces."

Elijah doesn't care about his shoelaces, but he ties them anyway. He nearly loses Danny in the airport rush. He doesn't care much about that, either, except for the fact that Danny has the money and the name of the hotel. (Typical.) Elijah nurtures a half-fantasy of disappearing into the crowd, making his own way to Venice, living by his wits for a week and then returning at the end of it all to share the flight home with his brother. He can't imagine that Danny would mind.

But Danny has stopped. Danny is waiting and watching – watching his watch, tapping his foot, prodding Elijah forward. International crowds huddle-walk between them. Families with suitcases. A girl who drops her Little Mermaid doll.

Elijah returns the doll and makes his way to his waiting

brother, who asks, "What took you so long?"

Elijah doesn't know what to say. Shrugs were invented to answer such questions, so that's just what Elijah does.

ITALY SHOULD MAKE DANNY FEEL RICH, BUT INSTEAD IT MAKES HIM feel poor. To change 120 (dollars) into 180,000 (lire) should make a man feel like he's expanded his wealth. But instead it makes the whole concept of wealth seem pointless. The zeros – the measures of American worth – are grotesque, mocking. The woman at the exchange bureau counts out his change with a smile – *Look at all the money you get*. But Danny would feel better with Monopoly chump change.

He leads Elijah out to the vaporetto launch. It's quite a scam they're running – the only way into Venice from the airport, really. It's one of the worst feelings Danny knows – the acknowledgment that he's going to pay through the nose, and there's nothing he can do about it.

"One hundred twenty thousand lire for the men," the vaporetto driver (the vaporetteer?) says in flawed English.

Danny shakes his head.

"Best price. Guarantee," the driver insists. Danny can tell he's been brushing up on his Best Buy commercials. Probably has his American cousins videotape them.

Danny tries three other drivers. Other tourists gratefully

take the vaporettos he discards.

"You really expect me to pay one hundred and twenty thousand lire – *eighty dollars* – for a vaporetto ride?" Danny asks the fourth driver.

"It is not a vaporetto. A *water taxi*, sir."

Elijah steps into the boat.

"Sounds great," he tells the driver. "Thank you."

I‍T IS POURING NOW. C‍OLD AND RAINY AND GREY.

Elijah can't see much through the clouds and mist. Still, he's thrilled by the approach – thrilled by the wackiness of it all. Because – he's realising this now – Venice is a *totally* wacky city. A loony idea that's held its ground for hundreds of years. Elijah has to respect that.

The buildings are *right on the water*. Elijah can't believe it. Sure, he's seen Venice in the movies – *Portrait of a Room with a View of the Wings of the Lady Dove*. But he'd always assumed that they picked the best places to show. Now Elijah sees the whole city is like that. The buildings line the canals like long sentences – each house a word, each window a letter, each gap a punctuation. The rain cannot diminish this.

Elijah walks to the front of the taxi and stands with the driver. The boat moves at a walking pace. It leaves a wider canal – Elijah can't help but think of it as an avenue – and takes a series of narrow turns.

Finally, they arrive at the proper dock. The driver points the way, and Danny and Elijah soon find themselves manoeuvring their suitcases through the alleys of Venice. The Gritti is smaller than Danny had pictured. He looks at its entrance suspiciously, while Elijah – unburdened by expectation – is more excited.

An elaborately dressed bellman glides forward and gathers their bags. Danny, momentarily confused, resists. It is only after Elijah says thank you that the suitcases are relinquished and the steps towards the registration desk are taken.

"May I help you?" an unmistakably European man asks from behind the counter. He wears an Armani smile. Elijah is impressed.

"Yes," Danny starts, leaning on the desktop. "The name is Silver. A room for two. Originally the room was under my parents' names, but they should have switched it to mine. Danny Silver. We need a room with two beds. On the canal side."

"If that's possible," Elijah adds. Danny swats him away.

The manager's smile doesn't falter. He opens a ledger and types a few keys on his computer. A temporary concern crosses his brow, but it is soon resolved.

"Yes, Silver," he says to Danny. "We have a room – a beautiful room. Two beds. That is what you requested in March. One room for Daniel and Elijah Silver."

Elijah thinks this sounds great. But Danny doesn't look happy.

"Wait a sec—" he says. "What do you mean, March? The initial reservation should have been for Rachel and Arthur Silver, not for Daniel and Elijah."

The manager checks the ledger again.

"We have no record of a change," he tells Danny. "Is this a problem?"

Danny shakes his head severely. "You see," he says to the man behind the desk, "my parents made me think this had been their vacation. But now you're saying that it was our vacation all along."

"Which is great," Elijah assures the still-confused manager. "It's just a surprise. For him especially."

"I see," the hotel manager intones, nodding solemnly. After the paperwork is completed, he produces a pair of golden keys. Elijah says thank you. Danny continues to shake his head and mutters his way to the elevator. The hotel manager smiles a little wider as he hands the keys to Elijah. Beneath his coutured appearance, his sympathy is palpable.

Elijah says thank you again.

"I can't *believe* it." Danny also can't stop hitting the side of the elevator.

"What's the matter?" Elijah asks as they walk to their room.

"What's the matter?!? They tricked us, Elijah. Our own parents. Tricked us. I mean, I knew they meant for us to come here together. But to have had that plan all along..."

They are being led into the room now. It is beautiful. Even Danny has to shut up for a second, just to look out the windows at the canal. Now that the rain has been reduced to a sound, it is moodily atmospheric, mysteriously foreign.

Elijah puts his suitcase on the bed closest to the windows as Danny tips (no doubt undertips) the bellman. When Danny returns to the windows, the spell has been broken. His tirade continues.

"I just can't believe they'd be so... manipulative. I can't believe they could stand there and lie to us, all these months."

"I think it's kind of nice," Elijah mumbles.

"What?"

"I said it's kind of a surprise."

Elijah knows, from years of practice, that it's best to just ride the conversation through. Unpack. Nod occasionally. Pretend that Danny's right, even if he's acting like he's been set up on a hideous blind date.

The trick is, Danny doesn't particularly like to hear himself talk, especially in monologues. Halfway through a sentence, he'll realise there's no reason to go on. His point has been made, if not accepted. Like now:

"If only they'd..." Danny says with a sigh. Then he pauses and listens to the rain outside. He realises he's in Venice, and that his parents cannot hear him. He walks to the closet and hangs up his coat. His last sentence dangles in the air, until it is forgotten.

NAPS AND DINNER. NAPS AND DINNER. IT SEEMS TO ELIJAH THAT every family vacation revolves around naps and dinner. This vacation does not appear to be an exception. As soon as Danny has unpacked, he kicks off his shoes and tears off the bedspread, thrusting it aside in a vanquished heap. They have just arrived – they have just been sitting for countless hours – and still Danny feels the need to lie down and close his eyes. Elijah is mystified. Danny's behaviour is perfectly predictable, and perfectly beyond understanding.

"I'm going for a walk," Elijah says.

"Be back for dinner." Danny nods for emphasis, then nods off.

Because the sky is grey and the time zones are shifty, Elijah finds it hard to gauge the hour. He never wears a watch (his own rebellion against time, against watching). He must rely on the concierge to supply him with a frame of reference. It is four in the afternoon. Two hours until dinner.

Upon leaving the Gritti, Elijah is presented with one of the most exquisite things about Venice – there is no obvious way to go. Although St Mark's Square pulses in the background, and the canals hold notions in sway, there is no grand promenade to lead Elijah forward. There is no ready stream of pedestrians to subsume him into its mass. Instead, he is presented with corners – genuine corners, at which each direction makes the same amount of sense.

Elijah walks left and then right. And then left and then right. He is amazed by the narrowness of the streets. He is amazed by the footbridges and the curving of paths. He sees people from his flight and nods hello. They smile in return. They are still caught in the welcomeness rapture; they've deposited their baggage, and now they wander.

We are like freshmen, Elijah thinks. The incoming class of tourists. The upperclassmen look at them knowingly, remembering that initial rush, when every moment seems picture-perfect and the tiredness distorts the hours into something approaching surreality.

Elijah feels giddiness and delight – although he is now in Venice, he is still high on the anticipation of Venice. The trip has not settled yet. It hasn't officially begun. Instead, Elijah is staking out the territory – sometimes circling the same block three times from different directions – somehow missing the major squares and the more famous statues. Instead, he finds a small shop that sells shelves of miniature books. The shopkeeper comes over and shows Elijah a magazine the size of a postage stamp. Elijah wants to buy it for Cal, but he's forgotten to bring money. He wants to come back tomorrow, but doesn't know if he will ever be able to find the store again.

He could ask for the address, but he doesn't want to travel in such a way. He wants encounters instead of plans – the magic of appearance rather than the architecture of destination.

Seconds pass with every door. Minutes pass with every street. Elijah never realises that he's lost, so he has no trouble finding his way back. Three hours have gone by, but he doesn't know this. Night has fallen, but that seems only a matter of light and air. When Elijah returns to the hotel, he doesn't ask the concierge for the time. Instead, he asks for a postcard. He draws a smile on the back and sends it to Cal. He cannot describe the afternoon any other way. He knows she'll understand.

Danny is still asleep when Elijah returns to the room. But only for a moment.

"What took you so long?" he asks, stretching out, reaching for his watch.

"Are you ready to go?" Elijah replies. Danny grunts and puts on his shoes.

Map in hand, Danny leads the way to St Mark's Square. His movement is propulsive, unchecked by awe or curiosity. He knows where he wants to go, and he wants to get there soon. Elijah struggles to keep up.

(*"What is taking you so long?"* Danny is on his way to the arcade and supposed to be watching his ten-year-old brother. Danny has agreed to drive Elijah and his friends to the movies and waits impatiently by the car. Danny is walking ten feet ahead to the bus stop and wants to get to his friends. Elijah is holding him back. That is the clear implication of the question. It is Elijah's fault. Elijah is left behind because he's too slow.)

As they approach St Mark's, the streets become more crowded. Danny weaves and bobs through the fray, dodging the men and women who walk at a more leisurely pace. Elijah follows in Danny's wake, without enough time to wonder if these couples are lovers, or if the children are playing games. Finally – too soon – they arrive at the Caffè Florian. Danny barks out their name and says, "Reservation, table for two." The maître d' smiles, and Elijah can sense him thinking to himself, *American*.

The restaurant unfolds like a house of mirrors – room after room, with Danny and Elijah stumbling through. Menus are procured, and the Silver brothers are shown to their table. Before he has even been seated, Danny orders wine and asks for some bread. Elijah studies his menu and wishes he knew more Italian.

The waiter is gorgeous – the kind of man, Elijah thinks, who would sweep Cal off her feet. It isn't just that he's beautiful but that his movements are beautiful. If all men looked like this waiter, there wouldn't be any need for colour – just white shirts and black pants, black shoes and black ties.

Danny is more interested in the waiter's grasp of the English language (mercifully adequate). Even though Elijah is a vegetarian, Danny does not hesitate to order a rack of lamb. Elijah tries not to notice and orders penne. When it is pointed out to him that the pasta course is an appetizer, he assents to a grilled vegetable plate. The waiter seems pleased, and Elijah is pleased to have pleased him.

"So what are we going to do?" Danny asks, breaking off a piece of bread and searching for the butter.

Elijah is not sure how big this question is. He assumes it is a matter of itinerary, not relations.

"I'd like to go to the basilica," he answers, "and the Academy."

"Well, of course. Those are givens. But what else? And where's the butter?"

Elijah points to the dish of olive oil. Danny is not pleased.

"I'll never understand why people do that – olive oil is so far removed from butter. It's a totally different sensory experience, you know? It's like substituting salt for cheese. Doesn't make any sense." Danny puts down the bread. "I'd like to go to the old Jewish ghetto tomorrow morning, if that's OK with you?"

Elijah is surprised. He had expected less of his brother – a search for the nearest Hard Rock Cafe, perhaps.

"We can go to the Academy when it opens," Danny continues, "and then take a vaporetto to the ghetto. The whole Sunday thing shouldn't be a problem there."

Elijah agrees, and is glad when the food comes – no need for further conversation. Which isn't to say the brothers don't talk. They do. But it's hardly conversation. Instead, it's filling the time with idle words – Danny returns to the topic of their parents' deception, and Elijah shifts gears by mentioning movies, one of the only things they can talk about easily. Even if Danny feels it's his masculine duty to disparage Merchant Ivory, at least it's something to talk about. Elijah realises this strain in conversation now, and Danny has the same thought a few minutes later. But there is no way for the two of them to know that they have this feeling in common. It doesn't come up at the dinner table, and instead the brothers teeter in their consciousness of being together, and apart. Danny takes out his Palm Pilot and shows Elijah all of the things it can do, most of them work-related. There is something about this that strikes Elijah as familiar – Danny always loved having the latest toys. Elijah tries to share in the marvel. The main course arrives, and he tries to avoid the sight of Danny gnawing at the bones.

They do not stay for dessert. By the end of the night, all they can say is how tired they've become.

On the walk back to the hotel, Elijah realises this is his first real adult trip. Even though he considers himself far from an adult, he can see that the trip marks some change. No parents. No teen tour counsellors. No teachers chaperoning. This is what adults do. They book tickets and they travel.

If Elijah is reluctant to see himself as an adult, or even as a potential adult, seeing Danny as an adult comes easily enough. In Elijah's eyes, Danny has always been a grown-up. Less of a grown-up than their parents, but still much more of a grown-up than Elijah's friends.

Danny was always so far ahead. None of Elijah's friends had a brother who was that much older. They would gather at the Silvers' house and become Danny's congregation, Elijah included. When they played basketball in the driveway, Danny always counted as four people, so the games were six on three, five on two, four on one. He always knew how to use the right curse words at the right time. If he wanted to change the channel, they would let him. Because he thought their shows were childish, and they didn't want to be childish. They wanted to know how to solve the secret puzzles the next few years would bring.

And then there was the armpit hair. Elijah spotted it one day when Danny was wrapped in a towel, finished with the shower. He raised his arm to deodorise – and there it was. Elijah told his friends, and the next time there was a pool party, Danny was the main attraction. He had no idea why the kids kept throwing the beach ball just over his head. Armpit hair was fascinating and scary and, more than anything, grown-up. Danny's voice was beginning to sound like he was chewing ice cubes. His body grew taller and taller, like celery shooting.

He was thirteen then, Elijah almost seven. Now, ten years later, Elijah realises he's older than Danny was. That all of those changes have happened to him, too. The changes that nobody has any say over. The biology – "growing" and "up" as a physical matter. The changes after – Elijah has to believe they're a matter of choice. Looking at Danny used to be like looking at the future. Now looking at Danny is like looking at a future he doesn't want.

His thoughts turn to Cal, to his friends, to home. He wishes that time was a matter of choice. That you could live your life controlling the metronome – speed it up sometimes, but mostly slow it down. Stay at the party for as long as you like. Prolong the conversation until everything is known.

To feel such a longing for his own life, even as he's living it – he wonders what that means.

ELIJAH FALLS ASLEEP AS SOON AS HE RETURNS TO THE HOTEL. IN FACT, he falls asleep a few turns from the hotel, but some mental and physical anomaly conspires to keep him upright until the door of the room closes. Danny is a little more fastidious before his own collapse. He hangs up all of his clothing and studiously brushes his teeth. Then he stands for a minute in front of one of the windows. He opens it wide, so the sounds of the canal and the laughter from the bar downstairs can segue into sleep.

Danny dreams of soldiers, and Elijah dreams of wings. They wake numerous times during the night, but never at the same time. Elijah thinks he hears Danny get up to shut the window, but when he wakes up, the window is still open.

Morning.

Breakfast.

"You fool," Elijah says, glancing at the menu.

"What?" Danny grunts.

"I said, 'You fool.'"

Danny looks at the menu and understands.

"No," he says, "I won't quiche you."

"Quiche me, you fool! *Please!*"

"If you say that any louder, you're toast."

"Quiche me and marry me in a church, since we cantaloupe!" Elijah is giddy with the old routine.

"Orange juice kidding?" Danny gasps.

"I will milk this for all it's worth."

"You *can't* be cereal."

"I can sense you're waffling..."

Danny looks up triumphantly. "There aren't any waffles on the menu! You lose!"

Elijah is surprised by how abruptly disappointed he is. *That's not the point*, he thinks. He turns away. Danny pauses for a second, watching him, not knowing what he's done. Then he shrugs, picks up an *International Herald Tribune*, and begins to read.

Danny and Elijah are both museum junkies, each in his own way. It is hard to entirely escape all vestiges of a shared parentage. From an early age, both of the Silver brothers found themselves folded into the backseat of the family car for Sunday-morning excursions to the museums of New York. There was never any traffic – driving through the city was almost like driving through a painting, the streets wider and cleaner than any New York street is supposed to be. An uncrowded city is a form of magic... and the magic only intensified as the museums neared. Sometimes the Silvers would walk amidst dinosaur bones and hanging whales. But most of the time, they made pilgrimages to colour and light, brushstrokes and angles. Elijah saved the buttonhole entry tags from each museum as if they were coins from a higher society – the nearly Egyptian M for the Met, the hip capitalisation of MoMA, each visit in a different colour from the time before.

Danny fell in love with *Starry Night* long before he knew he was supposed to. Elijah would bring his *Star Wars* figures to the MoMA sculpture garden and have Princess Leia and Han Solo make a home in the smooth pocket of a Henry Moore. As they grew older (but not too much older), the brothers would hatch Saturday-night schemes to make the museums their home. As their babysitter looked on with amusement, Danny and Elijah would pore over *From the Mixed-Up Files of Mrs Basil E. Frankweiler* as if it were both guidebook and bible – a map and a divination. Sometimes the museums' floor plans would also be consulted, the bathrooms carefully marked and noted. As the ten o'clock TV shows said their eleven o'clock goodbyes, Danny and Elijah would whisper their plans, each more elaborate than its predecessor. *We'll hide in the second-floor men's room, and when the janitor comes, we'll stand on the toilets so he can't see our legs. We'll hide under the bench in the room with the splatter painting. We'll spend the night in King Tut's tomb.*

The Sunday-morning trips began to ebb as Little League, summer camp, and adolescent resentment appeared. Danny became a teenager, which Elijah couldn't begin to understand. (Danny told him so. Repeatedly.) All plans were off, because Danny had new plans of his own. The Silvers still went to the museum together, but with the near-formality of a special occasion. These were Big Exhibition trips – mornings of Monet and afternoons of Acoustiguided El Greco.

Later on, Danny and Elijah made their own excursions into the city, sometimes with friends but most of the time alone. Danny loved MoMA, with its establishment airs and Big Artist dynamics. Elijah was more partial to the Whitney, with its Hopper despair and youth-in-revolt aspirations.

Strangely, neither Danny nor Elijah felt a strong affinity for the Met. Perhaps the Temple of Dendur fails to amaze after the twentieth visit. Perhaps the museum itself is too palatial, too expansive to ever really know.

It should be taken as a measure of Danny's true New York soul that his first reaction upon entering the Academy is a vow to spend more time at the Met, in the Renaissance rooms.

Elijah's response is a much more succinct (yet also more entire) "Wow."

There is a danger in living on a steady diet of Rothko and Pollack, Monet and Manet and Magritte. Danny and Elijah have an inkling of this now, almost immediately. They are struck, more than anything, by the details in the Academy's artwork. The faces in a painter's stonework. The downturn of a Madonna's eyes. The arrow's angle as it tears into Sebastian's side.

They do not know the stories behind all the paintings – such things weren't taught in Hebrew school. Perhaps that adds to the mystery and helps them approach in a strange state of wonder. Elijah is drawn to the paintings of Orsola – is she a martyr or a dreamer, a saint or a princess? He has no way of knowing. He asks Danny, and Danny mumbles something about enigmas. There is a happy complicity in their ignorance.

After an hour and a half, the Madonnas begin to look too much alike, and the Jesus babies are growing more grotesque in their bald adultness. Danny and Elijah are both losing sight of the details – it is harder to focus, and Danny is becoming restless. He wants to get to the synagogue in time for the noon tour. There will be more time for Art later.

They both agree on this.

A CITY PRESENTS MANY DIFFERENT FACES, AND IT IS UP TO THE traveller to assemble the proper composite. Venice seems, at first, to be a simple enough city to render. It is the canals, the basilica, the shutters on the homes. It is the gondolier's call and the beat of the pigeon's wing and the church bell that chimes to mark the passing of an hour. To many people, this is all, and this is enough. A tourist does not want to be weighed down by realities, unless the realities are presented as monumental stories.

It takes a traveller, not a tourist, to search for something deeper. Travellers want to find the wavelength on which they and the city connect.

Danny is drawn to the ghetto. None of his immediate ancestors ever set foot in Venice (or Italy, for that matter). None of his friends have ever spent time there. He has never read or dreamed about life in such a place. And yet this is the destination he has chosen within a city of destinations.

(Elijah comes too and is moved and affected, but not in the same way. This is not what he has visited for. For him, the city is much more elusive, and will not know where he wants to be until he actually gets there.)

According to the museum in the ghetto, eight thousand Italian Jews were sent to concentration camps during the Holocaust.

Only eight of them returned to Venice.

This is the fact to which Danny attaches himself. If the ghetto itself is the bell, this fact is the toll.

The word "ghetto" comes from the Venetian jeto, which means "foundry". The island upon which the Jews originally settled was formerly a foundry area (Danny learns). But the Jews, newly arrived from Germany and Eastern European countries, couldn't pronounce the soft j and instead called it geto. In the sixteenth century, the Jews were locked in from midnight to dawn; they became usurers because most other businesses were prohibited. (*Hence Shylock*, Danny thinks. *The Merchant of Venice* was the closest he came to finding meaning in Shakespeare in college.)

At one point in the ghetto, Jews had to wear yellow hats or scarves whenever they went out. Danny notes the colour yellow – how can he not? The past reverberates so clearly, later on. Yellow hats, yellow stars.

As Elijah waits in the courtyard, Danny stands in the shade of a Sephardic synagogue – still in use, saved from the World War II bombings by an ironic alliance made between the Germans and the Italians. People begin to gather for the tour – a small, quiet group, almost all of them American.

The inside of the synagogue is dominated by black woodwork and red curtains. There is a separate section for women – a shielded balcony, high beyond the pulpit. The guide jokes that this means women are closer to God. Only the men laugh.

The guide goes on to say that there are now 600 Jews in all of Venice. Danny feels his sombreness confirmed – how else can one feel when surrounded by such a majority of ghosts? You can find sorrow in the arithmetic, and you can find a bittersweet hope.

After the synagogue, Danny sees things differently. It's not that he's religious – at best, he would like to believe in God, if only he could believe it. Instead, his identity asserts itself. He sits in the plaza outside the temple and thinks about the 600 and what a crazy life they must lead. He wonders what it must be like to live in a place where Christ is in every doorway – well, maybe not every doorway, but he's sure it must seem that way. In American terms, it must be like living in the Bible Belt – with Christmas all year round.

Danny has these thoughts, but he doesn't share them. He can see that Elijah isn't in a similar space. Instead, he is sitting (shoelaces untied) in the sunniest corner of the plaza, watching a little redheaded girl in pink plastic sunglasses as she charges an unsuspecting flock of pigeons. There is a flash-flutter of wings – Elijah hunches over as the birds throw themselves skyward and fly thoughtlessly over the bench where he sits.

There is a small Judaica store open off the square. Danny walks to the window, but he doesn't go inside. Instead, he looks at the stained-glass kiddush cups and the tiny scrolls of the

81

translucent mezuzot. Women from the synagogue tour step inside the store and touch the cases reverently. Danny turns away. He wants to go inside, but he doesn't want to go inside. It's his place, but it's not his place. Elijah is walking over now, and Danny allows this to be a cue to leave.

They walk for some time without speaking. But this is a different non-speaking than it was before. Danny is still deep in his thoughts, and Elijah is letting him stay there.

Finally, Danny speaks, and what he says is, "It's incredible, really." Then he stops and points back to the synagogue and says he can't imagine. He just can't imagine. Elijah listens as Danny wonders how such things can happen, what lesson could possibly be learned.

"I don't know," Elijah says. He thinks of their parents, and how they'd be glad that their sons were here, thinking about it.

"All this history..." Danny says, then trails off. Lost in it. Feeling it connect. Realising the weight of the world comes largely from its past.

ALTHOUGH IT IS SUCH A SINGULAR WORD, THERE ARE MANY VARIATIONS of *alone*. There is the alone of an empty beach at twilight. There is the alone of an empty hotel room. There is the alone of being caught in a throng of people. There is the alone of missing a particular person. And there is the alone of being with a particular person and realising you are still alone.

Elijah parts with Danny in St Mark's Square and is at first disoriented. The courtyard is filled with thousands of people, speaking what seem to be thousands of languages. People are moving in such an everywhere direction that there is simply nowhere to go without firm resolution. Elijah's first instinct is to steal a quiet corner, to purchase a postcard from a hundred-lire stall and write to Cal about all the people and the birds and the way tourists stop to check their watches every time the bell tolls. He would sign the postcard *Wish you were here*, and he would mean it – because that would be his big threepenny wishing-well birthday-candle wish, if one were granted by a passerby. Cal would make him smile, and Cal would make him laugh, and Cal would take his hand so they could waltz where there was no space to waltz and run where there was no room to run. He thinks about her all the time.

Elijah finds a postcard and sits down to write, drawing a picture of the basilica above Cal's address. Then he files the postcard in his pocket for future delivery and wonders what to do. The alleys leave little room to think. So Elijah makes a decision not to decide. He steps into the crowd and gives in.

It is Elijah's rare talent – a talent he doesn't realise – to be surrounded by strangers and not feel alone. As soon as he steps into the rush of people, he is engaged. He is amazed through the power of watching, bewitched by the searching. As he is led from St Mark's to the walk beside the canal, he scans the crowd for beautiful people he will never know. He smiles as large groups struggle to stay together. Young children swoop beside his legs as old men lazily push strollers. Vendors sell the same cheap T-shirts at five-foot intervals. A band from a canal-side hotel plays, and mothers call their daughters away from the sea.

If you wanted to reassemble Elijah's afternoon, you probably could do it by stringing together all the photographs and all of the frames of videotape that he walks into. Always a passerby, he is immortalized and unknown.

Farther from St Mark's, the people fall away and the noise dies down. Strange sculptures appear – enormous anchors and acrobatic steel beams. Elijah figures these are just part of the landscape – the New City's wink at the Old City.

And then he finds the Biennial.

ONE NIGHT, DEEP IN DECEMBER, CAL HAD ASKED: "*DO YOU WONDER why we wander?*"

The answer, Elijah now realises, is: D*iscovery*.

In an age of guidebooks, websites and radio waves, discovery has nearly become a lost feeling. If anything, it is now a matter of expectations to surpass – rarely a matter of unexpected wonderment. It is unusual to find a situation that appears without word, or a place that was not known to be on the road.

As Elijah buys his ticket and enters the Biennial exhibition, he feels not only discovery but also a discovery of discovery. It's a spiritual rush, and it leaves him buoyant. He feels the antithesis of alone, because he is in the company of circumstance.

This is so cool, he thinks – this is his vocabulary of rhapsody. He has entered (for lack of a better reference) an Art World EPCOT Centre, each country's pavilion beckoning him forward. The afternoon is growing late, and the crowd has thinned out to a devoutly quiet core.

Elijah walks into the Spanish pavilion and stands before an abstract angel made from golden wire. Even though it doesn't move, Elijah can feel the angel lift. Serendipity is a narcotic, and

Elijah is under its sway. He stares at the angel until he can feel it watermark his memory of the day. Then, giddy and awed, he moves on.

Whether keenly striking or laughably awful, contemporary art is rarely unentertaining. Within its elaborately constructed pavilions, the Biennial demonstrates this appropriately. In Belgium, Elijah finds a series of open white (plaster?) containers. Luxembourg is populated by lawn chairs with the word "SAMPLE" placed in the corner (*perhaps*, Elijah thinks too easily, *they were desperate for artists from Luxembourg*). Holland features films of a girl flipping off a wall (her bloomers show) and of a man showering gratuitously. In addition, lightbulbs with nipples (there's no better way to describe them) litter the floor.

Elijah finds this more amusing than any so-called amusement park. Then he enters the strange world of the Japanese exhibit. Its lower level is devoted to repetitive photos of black-and-white cells. Elijah walks upstairs, and there is a burst of colour – brilliant spectrum cellscapes viewed from a wooden walkway on the outskirts of an inner lake. Elijah is dazzled. He goes through three times and then makes his way to the French pavilion, which is filled with smashed auto cubes.

Elijah wants to call Danny, because he feels it's near criminal to allow his brother to miss such a strangely magical place. But Elijah doesn't know the phone number of the hotel – he doesn't even know how to make a call from an Italian phone booth. So he vows to make Danny come tomorrow, and even decides to accompany him, if need be.

The epigram for the Russian exhibit is "Reason is something the world must obtain whether it wants to or not." At the centre of the pavilion is a container (large, metal) with a hole in it – the sign above it reads, *Donate for artificial reason*. Elijah reaches into his wallet and pulls out a crumpled American dollar. Then he moves on – to delicate paintings of violent acts and sculptured mazes scored by ominous music.

The narcotic of serendipity numbs his sense of time. The afternoon is over before Elijah has a chance to recognise it. An announcement is made in five languages – the exhibition will soon be closing. Elijah wanders to the gift shop and buys a few more postcards for Cal. Then he steps through the gate, back into the expected world. He looks to the exhibition sign and learns that the Biennial is closed tomorrow. Danny is out of luck. Elijah is disappointed. And at the same time, he is relieved. Not because the experience will solely be his (really, he wants Danny to see it). But instead because he knows deep in his heart that it would be foolish to return.

Discovery cannot be revisited.

"Do you wonder why we wander?" Cal had asked.

It was the night of the first snow; you could hear the branches bending and the icicles falling outside the window, beyond the wall.

They were warmth together. They were hot breath and blankets and wrapping themselves close.

And Elijah had thought, I *wonder why I never kiss you. I wonder what would happen*.

But he didn't say anything out loud.

Danny and Elijah had been walking the back way to school — even though Danny's first bell rang twenty minutes earlier than Elijah's, they usually walked together, with Danny dropping Elijah off at the playground before heading to middle school.

The back way went by the brook, by the strand of trees that the boys could call a forest without feeling any doubt. Sometimes along the way they found signs of trespass – teenage beer cans, hand-smashed or misplaced intact; gum wrappers folded into the ground; once, a high-heeled shoe.

That morning, they found a large spool of red twine. Elijah picked it up, the twine end pointing out like a tail.

"Let's tie the trees together," he suggested.

And Danny said, "Sure."

They tied the tail end to a branch – Elijah looping it like a shoelace, Danny double-knotting so it would hold. Then they ran randomly from tree to tree, sometimes throwing the spool high to get a branch that was just out of reach, other times dipping low to let the lowest of bushes in on the action.

They laughed, they looped, they were hopelessly late for school.

There was no way to explain it, so neither of them tried.

As Elijah wanders through the Biennial, Danny is in another part of town, altering his concept of nationality. At first, he thought he had it figured out: the American tourists were the loud walkers with Chicago Bulls T-shirts, and the Europeans were the teeter-walkers with an unfortunate propensity towards dark socks. But no. That was not the case at all.

Take baseball caps. Danny initially assumed that anyone wearing a baseball cap was from the U.S. – after all, baseball is not exactly America's most exportable pastime. But does that matter? No. Alongside postcards and Venezia T-shirts, street vendors are flush with New York Yankees, Washington Redskins and Dartmouth (*Dartmouth*?) paraphernalia.

Even in the Doges' Palace, things are askew. Danny stands beside an Ethan Hawke lookalike who is clearly a semester-abroad NYU student. Then Ethan opens his mouth and speaks an unintelligible language. Danny retreats to the side of a glamorous woman with a Spanish complexion and raven hair. She speaks fluent Brooklyn, albeit with a curator's vocabulary. (To her, the subtle curve of a David is a "mask-uline ref-rence to thuh fem-nin ark-uh-type.") Danny is confounded – the

Europeans are trying to be American, the Americans are trying to be European, and the Japanese are furiously upholding their stereotype by taking a horrendous number of snapshots for no clear reason.

Internationality is a German teenager in Venice wearing a Carolina Panthers jersey. (Danny passes three of them as he leaves the museum.)

And if this is internationality... where does that leave nationality? Danny has a fierce desire to identify Americans. Finally, he realises: you can tell an American not by the American-ness of his T-shirt but by the level of its obscurity. For example, if the shirt reads "Snoopy" or "New Jersey Sports" or (especially) "U.S.A.", odds are it's not an American. But if the shirt says "Lafayette College Homecoming Weekend" or "Paul Simon in Central Park", odds are it's an American in front of you.

Danny takes comfort in a stranger's Habitat for Humanity T-shirt as he walks back to the hotel. It is his way of keeping in touch with home.

Eᴌɪᴊᴀʜ ʟᴇᴀᴠᴇs ᴛʜᴇ Bɪᴇɴɴɪᴀʟ ᴀɴᴅ ᴡᴀʟᴋs sᴛʀᴀɪɢʜᴛ ɪɴᴛᴏ ᴀɴ ᴀᴅᴊᴀᴄᴇɴᴛ park. There are flowers everywhere. Elijah knows it's quite simple, but such things make him happy anyway. Old people sit on benches and talk boldly to one another. The women in particular make an impression on Elijah – old women in America don't seem as loud and animated and free. On the streets of Manhattan, it always seems like they travel alone, stooped, on their way from the grocery, towards somewhere equally unpleasant. But the Italian women don't look like abandoned grandmothers. They appear in flocks. They seem to know more.

Walking slowly, Elijah passes a man taking a picture of someone else's clothesline. It is, like all snapshots, a stolen image. The man clicks the shutter, then leaves guiltily.

The afternoon has now dimmed into evening. Candles are lit on cafe tables. The alleyways grow ominous, the crowds more unruly. It is as if twilight unleashes a darker undertow. Elijah feels the turn as the day goes from wistful to stark. The streets are so narrow they cry for confusion and claustrophobia. They desire speed, the rush of running through a maze. It is like a movie, Elijah thinks. A *James Bond movie*. There is no speed limit for pedestrians. It isn't like he's poolside – *no running allowed*. Unencumbered by packages, still high on the day, Elijah decides to bolt.

Bystanders are surprised. Elijah has been casually walking along. Now he runs as if he's being chased by KGB agents. It isn't entirely like a James Bond movie – he is careful not to knock down passersby or vendors of fruit.

As he gains speed, the streets seem to narrow further. The buildings threaten to cave in on him. The corners are sharper than before. The back of his coat trails in the air. Elijah wants to whoop with joy – running every which way, catapulting himself over bridges, a fascinating streak in a photo that will be developed weeks from now. He is tired, but he's free. He is living, because he's in motion.

Exhilaration.

Acceleration.

Exhilaration.

Acceleration.

Stop.

He almost runs into the wall of people. He is flying along, and then the crowd looms like a dead end. He could turn around, but curiosity encourages momentum. He touches the back of the crowd and then makes his way forward.

"Doctor? *Medico*?" a small female voice cries from somewhere in the front. Elijah pushes forward some more and then sees the girl and her distress. She is holding the same travel dictionary that Danny carries. "*Può chiamare un medico, per favore?*" From her accent, it's clear she took French in high school.

At her feet, a guy lies bleeding. Elijah steps back. He stares at the wound and then traces its trail to the pavement. The guy and the girl, both easily American, are no more than a year older than Elijah. The guy is bleeding, but he's also trying to smile. Elijah immediately feels a kinship and offers help.

He looks at the young man's wound. It doesn't seem too serious – the girl explains that he tripped on a wet stone and hit his head. She wonders whether he should be moved. No one in the crowd seems to have the answer – many are starting to walk away.

The young man rests his head on an L.L. Bean backpack. Elijah introduces himself and pulls a Kleenex out of his pocket to help stanch the flow of blood. The young man – Greg – is calmer than his partner – Isabel. As she frantically procures a handkerchief from a shopkeeper, he tells Elijah it's really not so bad.

"Liar," Isabel says. "The shopkeeper said help is on the way. Do you know what the Italian word for 'stitches' is? It's not in this stupid dictionary."

Just then, help arrives. Elijah almost laughs. The "ambulance" is a wicker chair placed on a wheeled cart. Elijah moves away from Greg as two men lift him into position. The blood has now spread over his shirtfront in baby-food dribbles. Despite his Eddie Bauer wardrobe, Greg looks like a bloodied prisoner being taken to the gallows. Isabel steps from one side of the chair to the other – she doesn't know where to be. Elijah hands her the backpack and stands to follow. But the paramedics are already on the move, with Isabel running hastily behind them. Greg looks over, one hand holding the Kleenex to his brow, the other hand raised in a Tom Hanks salute.

Elijah watches the chair disappear around a corner and immediately feels a loss. He can't believe that you can meet a person in this way and then lose touch with them forever. He could check all the hotels in Venice and look for a Greg and an Isabel, but he knows he won't. He wants to, though. Because he wants to believe in sudden fate.

The crowd has dispersed. People are obliviously stepping across the lines of blood, turning them into streaks and footprints. Those people who didn't see the incident look at the stain with disgust and dismay. Elijah just stares – his momentum is over, his giddiness lost. A hand touches his shoulder.

"I'm sure he'll be fine," a voice says. Elijah turns around, and there she is – easily one of the loveliest girls he's ever seen. She has short brown hair – light brown – and dazzling azure eyes. Her complexion is smooth. (Elijah, who never notices these things, not even when stoned, suddenly notices them now.) She isn't wearing any make-up. She looks twenty, give or take a year. And she is concerned about him. He sees that right away.

Elijah is afraid to speak, for fear that any word he says will come out as "uh".

"What you did was very nice," the girl continues.

"Thank you."

They hang on a pause. Elijah looks to the ground, looks back up, and she's still there.

A second pause will lead to departure. Elijah wants her to stay, so he gives her his name.

"I'm Elijah."

"Nice to meet you, Elijah. I'm Julia."

A bell chimes. Then three bells, and five bells, and seven bells at once.

It is six o'clock.

"Oh my God, I'm late!" Julia's eyes flash a genuine panic. Then they refocus on Elijah.

She touches his forearm.

"I'll see you soon. I promise."

And there is, that moment, a shock of recognition. Elijah doesn't even know yet what he is recognising. There is only the shock. The sense. That feeling of something happening that was meant to happen. Two people fitting in a space and time.

For a moment.

Julia smiles *sorry* at him and then is gone.

Elijah stands still. Julia is the kind of person who leaves a vapour trail. Traces of an accent, carried into memory. A perfume of kindness and expectation. A strange sense of certainty.

Elijah cannot explain it. The I'*ll see you soon* could be mistaken for a generic farewell. The I *promise* cannot be.

Julia knows she will see him soon.

He hopes she's right.

It is quiet when Elijah returns to the room. It is quiet, but not completely silent. Danny's breathing is as barely noticeable as the rise and fall of his body.

As Elijah steps gently over the floorboards, a bigger sound arrives. Underneath the hotel windows, a gondolier begins to sing with great passion, to cheers from all along the waterway. Elijah peers out and watches as other gondoliers move closer to be nearer to the first gondolier's boat. An accordion begins. Elijah opens a window wide. The only smell is the breeze. Even though the water is a churnish brown, for a moment Elijah can imagine it's a sapphire blue. That is how he feels. The gondolier is passing by, leaving the sound of the waves and an undertow from the Gritti's cafe.

This is why we go on holiday, Elijah thinks. *You can't get moments like this at home. The familiar can only bring another kind of wonderful.*

Even though the sun is lowering, even though there are dinner reservations to be upheld and clothes to change, Elijah lets Danny sleep. He pulls a chair to the window and takes Dickens' *Pictures from Italy* from his bag. He reads five pages and then, on his sixth page, he finds these words:

"Sunday was a day so bright and blue: so cloudless, balmy, wonderfully bright... that all the previous bad weather vanished from the recollection in a moment."

And Elijah thinks, *That is exactly it*.

The serendipity of the printed page.

Danny wakes up as Elijah turns the twenty-first page of that day. He is happy until he looks at his watch (sitting guiltily on the bedside table). Then he becomes frantic.

"Why didn't you wake me?" he accuses as he pulls on his pants. He can't help it – he feels sabotaged.

"I'm sorry," Elijah says in a tone that isn't sorry at all.

Danny hustles Elijah out of the room and orders the concierge to call the restaurant and pronounce a delay. Elijah is glad he spent the afternoon wandering, because Danny sprints him to the vaporetto so fast that there isn't much time to look at anything. Even on the boat, the air between them is tense and time-concerned. Elijah wants to let go of Danny's thoughts – after all, no amount of grimacing will make the boat go faster. But Danny's aggravation is inescapable. It imposes.

Elijah closes his eyes and thinks of Julia. He tries to count the number of words they exchanged – whatever the number is, it is unbelievably small. There is no real reason for Elijah to be thinking about her with such wistful longing. And yet, it is exactly because there's no real reason that the emotion is more intriguing.

After a time – a time filled with water and alleyways – they arrive at Antico Capriccio. It is a tiny restaurant, on the corner of somewhere and nowhere. It has been recommended by a friend of a friend of Danny's. He had to mention the friend of a friend's name when making the reservation – the Continental equivalent of a secret handshake.

They are greeted at the door by an old man named Joseph. It soon becomes clear that he is owner and waiter, maitre d' and busboy. Whenever possible, he stays out of the kitchen. That is his wife's territory.

Joseph doesn't speak much English, and doesn't care to hear it anyway. Danny starts to ask if Visa is accepted, but Joseph brushes the question away like a foul odor. Chatting amiably, he seats Danny and Elijah by an ancient fireplace. They are the only ones in the restaurant – or, at the very least, the only ones they can see. Joseph brings them wine before they even see the menus. Danny tries to protest – he prefers white to red. But Elijah takes the wine gladly; just the sight of it makes him feel warm.

The menus are entirely in Italian. Danny and Elijah both feel the need for Danny's travel dictionary, but they are too abashed to take it out. It doesn't matter anyway – when an answer isn't immediately forthcoming, Joseph pulls the menus from their hands and orders for them. He clearly revels in their confusion, but not in a mean-spirited, French way. *Let me take care of you*, his smile says. Elijah relaxes and submits willingly after it is made clear that he is *vegetariano*. Danny has never been able to submit willingly to anything besides his boss's whims. He is not about to start now. He asks if the fish is good. Joseph laughs and walks away.

"So how was your day?" Danny asks, his fingers tapping the table.

"Fine."

"Where did you go?"

"Around."

"The weather was good?"

"Yeah."

"It didn't rain?"

"Nope."

"That's good."

"Yeah."

Talking like this is like throwing small, round stones – nothing can be built from them, except perhaps the cairn of a lost conversation. Neither brother is trying. Instead, they are filling the space, united by their mutual dislike of awkward silence.

Joseph returns to light a candle. Elijah spots a medal on his lapel and asks if he's ever been in a war. This is clearly the right question to ask. Joseph takes the medal from his jacket and lets Elijah hold it in his hand. In a river of Italian broken by crags of English, he talks about his days in the military – *il paese*, *il fiume*, *la morte*. Elijah hears the word *diciannove*, but cannot tell whether it is an age or a number of years.

As Joseph leaves to compel the first course, Elijah finds himself thinking once more about Julia. It surprises him – to be hearing an old man's reminiscence of the war one moment, and to be recalling her eyes in the next. The segue is in the storytelling – he sees Joseph's words as something he wants to share with Julia. He doesn't know whether he'll ever see her again, but still he feels the need to tell her things.

How strange, he thinks. *How very strange.*

His hope to see her again is prayerful – not because it is addressed to a spirit, but because it is mysteriously drawn from an unknown part of his soul.

My soul. How very strange.

"So how's your girlfriend?" Danny asks. Elijah is jarred – how could Danny know about Julia – and why would he call her that?

Danny sees the confusion on Elijah's face and tries again. "You know – what's her name – Cat?"

"Cat?"

"You know, the girl you hang out with."

"Oh. Cal."

"Yeah, Cal."

"She's not my girlfriend."

"Whatever you say."

Elijah thinks about Cal and feels a vague sort of distance. For the first time, she seems out of reach. All of their Wonder Twin Telepathic Powers have failed him. *"Whenever you need me,"* she'd say, *"wiggle your ears."* Elijah never had the heart to tell her he couldn't wiggle his ears. He'd just smile and nod, and know (wiggle or not) they would never have distance, even when they were apart.

But now – what does it mean? Cal is suddenly a home-movie presence. The feeling of non-feeling is inescapable. Elijah assumes it will pass. He reasons it out – in a corner of a restaurant in a corner of a city, it is natural to feel Away and Apart. As soon as he gets back to the hotel, he'll be able to pull out his Magic 8 Ball keychain and conjure Cal from the radio-waved ether. Simple as that.

As Elijah drifts off and Joseph mercifully brings the first course, Danny's thoughts also turn to the distance from home. He thinks about voice mail and conference calls, even though he hates himself for doing so. He's not so far gone that he doesn't know such thoughts are inappropriate. But such thoughts bring urgency to his life. Without them, he would have no clear game to play.

"Remind me to call Allison when we get back to the hotel," he tells Elijah.

"Allison?" Elijah echoes with a distinct question mark.

"Yes. She's working on the ranch-dressing account with me. I need to check in with her. See what's going on."

"Oh." Elijah's curiosity deflates.

"We're supposed to get the shooting script in for this great ad. Spike Lee might direct it."

"Oh."

You'd think I had the most boring job in the world, Danny sighs to himself. *You'd think I was an accountant. Or a dentist. I mean, Spike Lee's a big deal. Advertising is as creative as being a snotty English-major-in-training.* Elijah's problem, in Danny's mind, is that he has no sense of what it takes to make a living.

Danny's problem, in Elijah's mind, is that he has no sense of what it takes to make a life.

When Danny mentioned Allison's name, Elijah had been hoping she was a girlfriend. Danny used to have dozens of girlfriends, most of them nicer to Elijah than Danny himself. In high school, Marjorie Keener had brought along an extra flower for Elijah when she picked Danny up for the prom. Angelica, Danny's freshman-year college girlfriend, had spent most of their spring break playing Boggle with Elijah until the wee hours of the morning. (Danny never played, because Danny always lost.) Sophie – from junior year – had been cool, even if Elijah had spotted her eating disorder before Danny ever noticed. That relationship didn't last very long.

Now Danny didn't have anyone. He had Allison – an office full of Allisons. No doubt the only thing he ever shared with them was an elevator ride.

"So how's your job going this summer?" Danny asks. He's already plowed through his pasta. Elijah has taken two bites.

"It's OK," Elijah replies. He'd almost forgotten about working in his school's admissions office. It was that kind of job.

"So you sort through applications?"

"Nah. We just file last year's applications. There was this one girl – she painted her whole room the school colours and sent in a photo with her holding a paintbrush. Just to get in."

"Did she get in?"

"Yes, actually."

"And that's all you do all day – file? Will that get you into college?"

"Well, we can't all be in *advertising*."

"What is *that* supposed to mean?"

"Nothing."

Elijah bends back over his pasta. Danny tries to signal Joseph for more wine, but Joseph is nowhere to be found.

Danny and Elijah are both struck by the abruptness of their conversation. They both know they've gone a little bit too far. They've broken their unwritten agreement – they are allowed to gibe each other, but it's never supposed to get too personal.

Danny had always been too old to beat up Elijah. Even to a ten-year-old, a seven-year difference seems unfair. Danny was not above using force to get his way – an arm twist for the remote control or a shove to get the front seat. But it was not the habitual violence symptomatic of a usual brother-brother relationship.

Instead, Danny showed Elijah the depth of his disdain. There were times of pure love, for sure. But when Danny wanted to strike out, he did it with a shrug, not a fist. If he wanted to, he could pretend Elijah wasn't there. Elijah could preen or caterwaul – whatever he did, he only made it worse in Danny's eyes. Eventually, Elijah gave up. He found his own private universe. And he learned his own form of disdain.

The bad can be found in anything. It is so much easier to find than the good. So when Elijah hears *advertising*, he thinks *sellout* and *phony* and *liar*. Most of all, he thinks, *My brother is so different from me. He is so wrong.*

And when Danny hears *I'm going to be an English major when I get to college*, he thinks *pothead fallback* and *no sense of reality* and *penniless*. He thinks, *Anything but me.*

Perhaps Joseph senses this divide as he brings the main course. He has brought them different dishes, but knows they will not share. There is sadness in his eyes, because he knows they will not experience the full joy of the meal.

The meal is, in fact, one of the best they've ever had. Even Elijah, who never thinks of food as something that can be enjoyed like a CD, is enraptured.

It is an experience they will talk about for years to come. And, more important, it is a meal they can talk about for the rest of the evening, all the way back to the hotel.

Elijah is nervous when the time comes to pay the check and leave the tip. But Danny surprises him by leaving thirty per cent. They both chorus Joseph with thank-yous before they leave into the night. Joseph smiles and pats the two brothers on the back. He watches as they slowly walk to the vaporetto station. Then he returns to their table and pushes the chairs together before he leaves.

THEY ARE DUE TO VISIT MURANO THE NEXT MORNING.

Elijah cannot believe it is already their last day in Venice. He feels like he's only just arrived. The prospect of Florence (and furthermore Rome) excites him, but not as much as before. It is the traveller's great dilemma. When he arrived, Elijah had felt he was wandering over vast sands. Now he realises he's been in an hourglass the whole time.

Will that get you into college? – Danny's words from last night. His question. The ever-present question.

The applications lie in unopened envelopes. Cal has put them in alphabetical order on his desk. She scribbles comments under the postmarks, the things she's found from visits he hasn't made, information sessions he hasn't even considered.

He knows he's supposed to hate high school. Everybody says they hate high school. The cliques, the insecurity, the pressure. But Elijah has somehow found a place that he loves. It is not childhood. It is not adulthood. It is now, and it too resides in the hourglass.

He'd chosen a high school his brother had never been. Teachers who had never heard Danny's name. Hallways that wouldn't bear his echo. He hadn't been sent away, although maybe he'd made it sound that way to the friends he was leaving back home. But he had wanted to go. He had wanted to live there and sleep there and wake there. He had wanted to be somewhere entirely new. Not because of Danny or his parents, who were at first a little sad about him going away, but then felt better when he said it was about getting a different experience, not about escaping. Funny, but at the time it had seemed like a grown-up thing to do. *Planning for your future*, his father had said. Once he got there, though, the future was the last thing on his mind. When he went home to his parents and his old friends, that was the past. And Cal and Ivan and the others were the present. The future? Maybe Danny was the future. But less so. The avoidable future.

Elijah lies awake for an hour before he rises from the hotel bed. He drifts from the past to the near past. He wishes memory could be as easy as breathing.

Thoughts of Julia begin to blur within the air.

The sound of small waves seems to bring on the daylight.

Danny has trouble waking up. The time zones have finally caught up with him. Reluctantly, he gets dressed and plods his way to breakfast with Elijah. He realises he has become a full member of the Society of Temporary Expatriates – the dining area is filled with people from their flight or from the synagogue or from loud American conversations on the street. Danny feels a displaced sense of community. Even on the vaporetto ride to Murano, he spots a teenager from the plane, who was wearing a Wolverines T-shirt yesterday and now pledges sartorial allegiance to the Bulls.

Murano is an island known throughout the world for its glass. Danny is surprised to find that most of its buildings are stone. With jet-lag weariness, he allows himself to be led to kilns and hammerings. He admires without touching. He is amazed when colour appears from the wand of the glassblower. He expects to find the glass clear, but instead discovers it rimmed with red or blue.

By the third stop, Danny is ready to leave. He feels very much like his reflection – worn out and only vaguely present. Elijah is kept awake by his wonder. Danny subsides.

"A nap," he says. But Elijah isn't listening. He is looking around, as if for someone else.

"Who are you looking for?" Danny asks.

"No one," Elijah replies, focusing now.

Yeah, right, Danny thinks. He figures his brother is looking for some old lady he helped to cross the street. Or maybe that girl from the plane who wouldn't shut up about herself.

"Do you want to go back for a quick nap before we leave?" Danny asks, even though it's only eleven.

Elijah nods. He wants to go back.

But he doesn't have any intention of napping.

THE LAWS OF GRAVITY VARY FROM CITY TO CITY. IN VENICE, THE LAWS state that no matter where you want to go, you will always be drawn back to St Mark's Square. Even though you know it will be immensely crowded, and even though you have nothing in particular to do there, you will still feel yourself drawn.

Elijah diverges from Danny at the gates of the hotel and finds himself gravitating. He moves as if he knows the place. It is a spiritual familiarity.

Past the coffee bars and through the crowds of pigeons, Elijah heads for the basilica. It is busy, as it always is. There are numerous signs prohibiting photography. Some tourists rankle at this and fail to put their cameras away. Others would never imagine taking a photograph in such a place. They stand solemnly before the statues and say prayers of thanks or pain.

Elijah pays his admission and walks into the entryway. Immediately he is amazed by the floors. Marble of every colour – triangles and squares dancing in greater shapes. As others rush past, Elijah kneels down. He runs his hand over the marble. Other people stop to watch him, and it is only then that they too see the floors. Elijah is overwhelmed by the sheer fact of all the people who have walked over this very spot. As he watches Nikes and loafers glide past, he tries to fathom the feet of centuries ago. A person could stay in this same place his whole life and meet millions of people from all over the world. But instead, everyone moves on, and meets no one.

From the floor, Elijah looks to the ceiling – all gold tile and mural, epic scenes and godly interventions. The ceilings speak a different language from the floors. Both are art, but the ceilings are story while the floors are mathematic. People walk between, every single one of them a foreigner.

Elijah stands back up and re-enters the flow. He veers towards the corners, delicate shrines that counterbalance the immensity of the building. He stops in front of a saint he doesn't know. Candles flicker at her feet. Elijah loves the ceremony of candles – his mother waving her hands over the flames on Shabbat, or the two memorial candles that beacon through the house on Yom Kippur. This is, of course, a different context. Yet Elijah is tempted to light a candle, just the same. He puts three thousand lire in the box and pulls a candle from its stand.

He'll light one for Cal. She's Christian, so that must be legal.

He wonders what she'd wish for. He wonders what she'd want to tell the saint.

He touches the wick against another candle. He wonders if its wish transfers with the flame.

The wax drips on to his hand. An old woman shuffles up and takes a candle for herself.

Cal. Cal. Cal.

"Happiness," Elijah whispers. Then he places the candle at the altar. The wax cools on his hand as he pulls away.

The old woman lights her candle, and a smile flickers across her face. Elijah thinks of birthdays and wonders why birthday wishes aren't made when the candles are lit. If he could have his way, candles would never be blown out.

After a few minutes of candle staring, he drops some extra coins into the candle box. Not for the candle, but for all candles. No payback necessary.

Back at the hotel, Danny realises too late that it's too early to take a nap. He wrestles across his bed and tries to contort himself into sleepfulness, but it's no use. After a half hour of impatient waking, Danny shifts to the side of the bed and picks up the phone. It takes a showdown with a contentious operator (who seemingly wouldn't know an AT&T calling card if it rode a gondola up to her desk) for Danny to place a call to his voice mail. There are nine new messages, which makes Danny happy, even as he mentally chastises all the people who have left him messages when his outgoing message clearly states that he is away.

*4 *to save*, *6 *to delete*, *1 *to respond*. These dialing commands have become an essential part of Danny's being, his voice-mail mantra. Even after a live phone conversation, Danny finds himself hitting *6 to erase what he's just heard. Now he plows through the messages with corporate efficiency. He is happy to hear that there aren't any emergencies, and he is happy to hear that not much else is happening, either. Message six is from Cody in Legal, who informs Danny that one of his catchphrases has just been registered for trademarking. Danny smiles at that and forwards the message to Allison. He tells her he loves to be working in a country where the phrase "All the Oil You Need" can be owned.

After listening through the messages (sometimes twice), Danny faces a different set of options. *1 *to record a message*, *8 *to change a message*, *3 *to listen to saved messages*. Danny *1s his work-friend John, just to say hey. Then he *1s Allison to tell her all is well and that he hopes work isn't too chaotic with him gone. As soon as he's hit the # key to end, he realises he has something more to say, so he *1s her again and tells her he hopes she's not working too late. Then he phones his assistant and says the same thing. He thinks about *1ing Gladner or Gladner to thank them for the time off. But even he sees how ridiculous this would sound, especially since they've sent him away to think of things other than work.

Impulsively – reluctant to hang up quite yet – Danny hits *3. Then he lies back on the bed and closes his eyes.

You have eight old messages, the voice-mail femail says. *Your first message is one year, five months and twelve days old.*

Cue: The Twilight Zone theme. Starting with a click of the tape recorder, then growing louder.

"Yes, folks, we've entered a world of bright lights and big cities... a world of wine, women, and thongs... a world where debutantes still roam the SoHo plains in search of the perfect two-hundred-dollar T-shirt bargain. Yes, we have entered... the Danny Zone! Do-do-do-do Do-do-do-do. My name is Enigo Montoya, but you can call me Will for short. I will soon be entering the Danny Zone and need to arrange the peculiars. So PLEASE give a call back at 415-66 – hell, you can

use your ESP to complete the number. I eagerly await your call. If you don't call back in fifteen seconds, I will self-destruct. Fifteen. Fourteen. Thirteen..."

One year, five months and twelve days old. Which would make it one year, five months and two days since he last saw Will, his best friend in the whole wide world – until the whole wide world intervened. He had flown in five days after the message, while Danny was caught in a tempest of work.

"Can you make time?" Will had asked.

"I can't make time," Danny had responded, "but if you know someone who does make time, I'd be more than happy to buy a lot of it from him."

Before the call, it had been another year since they'd seen each other. In that year, Danny had stayed in the same place and had progressed in the same job. Will had lived in Spain, Nebraska and California. He'd been a playwright, a computer consultant and a door-to-door salesman. He had a million stories to tell. Danny only had one or two. He didn't want to bore Will with the details of his work, and at the same time he resented the way such details became boring. Will wanted to stay up late and go to clubs where the barmaids were playfully cruel. He wanted to hit galleries and pawnshops and diners where a grilled cheese still cost two dollars and the tomato came free. Danny didn't know such places. After two days, he felt he didn't know the city at all.

"What have you been *doing*?" Will asked with mock exasperation.

And the only answer Danny could think of was, *Living my life.*

Will wanted Danny to cut work. Danny felt he couldn't. Will wanted Danny to get a tattoo. Danny wouldn't.

They parted on good terms, but it felt like parting, and it felt like terms. Danny hadn't meant to lose touch with Will – but all it took was one lost change-of-address card and the fact that Will refused to have e-mail. Danny heard word through friends of friends – Will was now a potter in Oregon – but he knew it wasn't enough to send word back. After all, Will knew where Danny was. It wasn't like he'd moved.

*Please press *4 to save, *6 to delete, or *7-3 to listen to this message again*, the voice-mail femail insists. Danny hits *4.

*1 – to respond – is only an option for internal calls.

WHILE DANNY DIALS TRANSATLANTIC, ELIJAH WALKS TO THE TOP OF the basilica. Not to the dome, but to the balcony. Touched full-force by the sun, he watches over the square, tourists moving like rivulets of water, birds shifting like newsprint fingerprints. A string band concertos to the left, while a trumpeter blasts from the right. Strangely, the two sounds complement rather than conflict.

The bell tower begins to ring. The time is marked.

Elijah breathes. He breathes deeply and tries to pull his sight into his breath, and his hearing into his breath, and his feeling into his breath.

He knows this will be his goodbye to Venice. The rest will be walking and packing and checking out. This is the height. This is the time for thanks.

He thinks of Julia, the stranger, and says goodbye to her as well.

He thinks of Julia, and she appears.

She doesn't see him at first. She steps out on to the balcony and walks to the edge. She leans against the railing and dangles her head over. She is smiling at the square, like a child tummy-down on a swing, pretending to fly.

Elijah knows he is not part of this picture. He knows he is seeing more of her than he would be brave enough to give of himself.

Wonder lights her face. She stands up straight again and shakes her head in a barely perceptible motion. She is watching sunset, even though the sun is still high in the sky.

Then, with another shake of her head, she moves a step back. Her smile is now self-aware. She knows she is a bit loony in her wonder, but she doesn't really mind.

Elijah walks over before he can think about it. He walks over because what he feels is strange enough to be a dream, and in dreams ordinary rules do not apply.

"Hello again," he says.

She turns to him and looks momentarily surprised. Not displeased. But surprised.

"Hello," she says. "Isn't this wonderful?"

He looks back over the square.

"Absolutely."

"It makes me want to—"

"—fly?"

Julia laughs. "Yes! Exactly! How did you know what I was going to say?"

And the answer is: *Because I was going to say the same thing.*

Elijah feels the electric rush that comes when coincidence turns into coinciding. He feels nervous and comfortable, disbelieving and amazed.

He does not need to know what is happening in order to know something is happening.

"Where are you from?" he asks.

"Toronto," she replies, her inflections now explained.

"Have you been here long?"

"No. You?"

"No."

They are not looking at each other. Instead, they stare out into the square, each extremely aware of the other's every breath, every move.

This doesn't make sense, he thinks.

Her arm brushes his, and when she turns to see him, loose strands of her short hair blow over her eyes.

"I'm going to Florence," he says.

And she says, "I am too."

FLORENCE

Since Danny can stand Elijah's driving even less than Elijah can stand Danny's, it is Danny who drives the rent-a-car. Within five minutes they are lost on a road where it's prolongedly impossible to make a U-turn. In response, Danny swears like a drag queen with a broken heel as Elijah bends and folds the map into something approaching origami.

It is not a good moment.

Danny swerves through the lanes, dodging the European cars that whiz by at incomprehensible speeds. Elijah wonders how guilty his parents will feel when both their sons get trapped in a fiery wreck in the middle of a prepaid vacation.

We are going to die, Elijah genuinely thinks. *Or, at the very least, we are going to kill a cyclist.*

He takes some comfort in the fact that the stop signs still read STOP.

Eventually, the road they're on turns into the road they had meant to get on in the first place. Once on the highway, Danny relaxes behind the wheel. Elijah puts a CD in the stereo – Paul Simon's *Graceland*, something they can agree upon.

Once the music is in, Elijah decides to close his eyes.

If he can't see, he won't be scared.

He thinks of Julia and the hour they'd managed to steal before Elijah had to leave Venice. A spare cafe hour of signals and conversation, sharing the arcane facts of their lives, touching upon the founding of Rhode Island and the temperature of a Toronto summer day. Finally, he'd had to leave, their goodbye drawn out over a number of goodbyes and one-last-things to say. He didn't know where he'd be staying in Florence, but she had been able to write down the name of her *pensione*. He promised to be there as soon as she arrived.

Danny had not been happy when Elijah returned so late. When Danny demanded to know why he was so tardy (such a schoolteacher word), Elijah disguised Julia in a fit of mumbles and evasions, saying quite simply that he'd been lost. Danny could believe this easily enough.

Now they are making up for Elijah's delay, as Danny fulfils all of his test-drive fantasies. Even with his eyes closed and the music playing, Elijah can sense the impatient speed. There are two kinds of drivers, he thinks: those who see the world around the road, and those who fixate on the road itself.

We'll end up where we want to be. We always do.

Elijah reclines in the melody of "Under African Skies" and thinks once more of Julia. The promise of Florence has become the promise of their next encounter. But unlike Danny, he is not in a rush. He wants to feel the nervous sweetness of expectation, if only for a little while longer.

"**O**PEN YOUR EYES."

Elijah hears Danny's voice and wants to reject it. He's been safely, happily asleep, dreaming of a gondolier who sings love songs to a maiden on a bridge. Surely, Danny doesn't need to wake him. Surely, he can read his own map. Why can't he leave Elijah to his reverie?

"I mean it. Open your eyes."

Elijah stirs and groans. He opens his eyes and sees the plastic wood of the dashboard. *Graceland* has now played twice around.

Danny smiles in amusement and says, "Look outside."

Elijah turns to the window and is startled straight into joy. A field of sunflowers surrounds the road, devout yellow heads bent, an oceanic congregation. Elijah cannot see beyond them. There are so many, and they are all so bright. Sunflowers as far as the eye can see.

"I wonder," Danny says, "are sunflowers called sunflowers because they look like the sun, or because they follow the sun? Either one would be a perfectly good explanation, and there are so few things that deserve two perfectly good explanations."

The sunflowers are retreating now – Elijah turns back to look at them, his wonder nearly dreamlike in its intensity and disbelief. He feels a strange gratitude towards his brother, for he knows he could have slept through the whole thing.

So instead of answering Danny's question, he says, "I met a girl named Julia in Venice." And he tells a little bit of the story. Not the good parts. But enough to let Danny know what's going on.

A GIRL, DANNY THINKS. *ELIJAH HAS MET A GIRL.*

He doesn't know how he feels about this.

FLORENCE IS NOT QUITE WHAT DANNY OR ELIJAH HAD BEEN EXPECTING. Venice, in many ways, has misled them into thinking that the past can remain fully intact. And yet here is Florence, a city of the past with a city of the present imposed right atop it. (The future is nowhere to be found.) Benettons grow in the cracks between cathedrals. Moped-clad citizens run on caffeinated fumes. Crosswalks are suddenly necessary. Ghetto-blaster teenagers skateboard past multinational newsstands. The Arno River shrugs by.

For a moment, traffic makes Florence seem like anywhere else. As Danny curses and stops and starts and struggles for direction, Elijah takes drive-by snapshots of the city and its contradictions. Venice was a museum city; Florence is a city with museums. There is, Elijah thinks, a big spiritual difference between the two.

Danny and Elijah are staying a little outside the city, at the Excelsior on the Piazza Ognissanti. There is a message waiting for them at the desk. Elijah's heart lifts when he sees the envelope, wondering how Julia could have known.

But the message is from Mr and Mrs Silver – *Hoping you're having a lovely time!* – signed with *Much Love*. Danny grumbles a little (he still has not entirely forgiven his parents' trickery) and hands Elijah the note. The porter brings their bags to the room, and they immediately depart. (Elijah takes a piece of the hotel stationery with him, just so he'll know where he's staying.)

Elijah wants to track Julia down immediately. But Danny is so antsy that he's willing to forgo his afternoon nap. This day is not supposed to be a Transportation Day – it is supposed to be a Florence Day, and Danny is willing to take the necessary steps to see it before sundown.

They taxi to the centre of the city in the most rushed hour of the day. Danny is reminded of home – men with their leather briefcases jostle down the sidewalk, exuding a barely concealed hostility. A woman with a stroller crosses against traffic; horns blare in response.

"Where have you been?" the taxi driver asks. "Where are you going?"

Danny looks down and notices Elijah's shoes are untied.

"You'd better tie them," he says.

Elijah scowls and makes a double knot.

The driver nods and turns up the radio.

Elijah stares out the window, somehow expecting Julia to be there, waving.

THE DUOMO IS CLOSED, SO ELIJAH AND DANNY MUST BE CONTENT with walking around its brilliantly traceable exterior.

"Not bad, for a church," Danny says. Elijah is elsewhere.

"Where's she staying?" Danny asks.

"Here," Elijah replies, pulling out an old bank receipt with an address written in red ink on the back.

"Then I guess we'd better go there and ask her to dinner."

It is, by all means, an awkward situation. Because Elijah has no intention of sharing his time with anyone but Julia. But at the same time, he must be grateful for his brother's gesture. As they wait in the lobby for Julia to appear, Elijah tries to conjure somewhere else for Danny to go. But it's no use... for now.

The elevator teasingly discharges passengers who are markedly not Julia. Danny laughs to himself as they disembark, imagining that one of the sixtysomething dowagers is the woman for whom Elijah has so obviously fallen. He almost doesn't notice when Julia arrives. It's from Elijah's beaming that Danny can tell.

So this is Julia, he thinks. She isn't really attractive – rather boyish, with her hair so short and no make-up. No breasts to speak of. In fact, no real curves of any kind. And what is a girl without curves if not, well, a boy? Danny is confounded by his brother's choice.

"Julia, this is my brother, Danny. Danny, this is Julia." She doesn't have a label yet. She is just Julia.

"Nice to meet you."

"Nice to meet you."

Elijah doesn't know what to do. He doesn't know what to say, doesn't know where to put his hands, doesn't know how familiar to be with Julia, especially with Danny watching. Julia sends him a winking look – something for them to share – and suddenly Elijah feels OK with the situation. Danny is harmless. Julia is everything.

It is, by European standards, obscenely early for dinner – not yet seven o'clock. This makes it easier for them to change their reservation from two to three. It also ensures that the few other people in the restaurant will be English-speakers like themselves.

Even though most of the tables are empty, they are seated right next to a family of six. Their acquaintance is soon enough made – the youngest child, age three, grabs Elijah's shirt as he goes to sit down. The mother apologises profusely, while Elijah profusely declares that it's no problem whatsoever. Soon enough, introductions are made, and Mrs Allison Feldstein of Commack, Long Island, is telling the story of the Feldstein family's day in Pisa:

"We were worried that we'd be driving all that way for nothing – like those poor souls who drive halfway through South Dakota to see Mount Rushmore. You know what I mean? But Davey has a Sno-globe collection – don't you, Davey? – and he really wanted to have one from the leaning tower. And there's a restaurant two towns over from ours named The Tower of Pizza, so the kids wanted to go on account of that, ha ha. So we got in the car and drove there – it wasn't as long as we thought it would be. The drive was actually enjoyable. And when we got there, the town itself was a very pleasant surprise. It's so strange to see something in person that you've been seeing all your life. I mean, everyone knows the tower leans. But it's not until you're standing right there that you can truly understand what a spectacular kind of thing this is. It's really quite striking, especially when you're looking at it from behind. I mean, buildings just aren't meant to lean away from you, so it's startling when they do. The little one here was terrified it would fall, and I have to tell you, the thought crossed my mind too. It probably crosses everyone's mind. It shakes the fundamental trust we have in buildings. And it's a beautiful building – that's something you never hear about. It would be worth seeing even if it wasn't leaning. And the cathedral next to it – who even knew there was a cathedral? But it's really one of the most striking ones we've seen. It was all white and shadow. I loved it. And believe you me, we've seen more than enough cathedrals on this trip..."

As Elijah listens to this, Danny shoots a look at Julia – who rolls her eyes right back. They have become prisoners of Jewish Geography, inextricably bonded to these similar strangers in a strange land.

Mrs Feldstein's children grow restless before either she or Elijah does. They are swapping itineraries – the Feldsteins are on their way to Venice and have just come from Rome. Danny begins to play with the remnants of bread on the tablecloth. Julia laughs at this and begins to flick crumbs his way. Elijah turns back to the table aglow with conversation – only to find his brother and his newfound love skirmishing playfully. It is the first time in a long time that he feels like the more mature brother.

As soon as he's back, Julia's attention returns to him, and he feels all right again. Danny feels the centre slip away from him. He is once more a hypotenuse.

"How was your drive?" Julia asks, and even though it could be meant for either of them, both of them know it is Elijah's place to answer.

"Fine," Danny says.

"If your idea of 'fine' is being trapped in a car with the Red Baron driving," Elijah adds.

"You're mixing your transportation metaphors."

"It's not a *metaphor*, it's a *reference*."

Julia smiles. "I think I'm getting the picture," she says, and the two of them are reduced to silence.

"You'll have to pardon us – we're brothers," Danny says after a moment.

"Yes, I've noticed. I have four brothers of my own."

Four brothers. Neither Danny nor Elijah can imagine having four brothers. Separately, they wonder if it's harder or easier than having just one.

From this point on, Julia owns the conversation. Elijah admires the fact that she is charming enough to make the people she is with act charming as well. Danny's and Elijah's words suddenly run in paragraphs, not sentences. They tell her of their parents' trickery, of their lives back home. Danny talks about work, and even Elijah isn't bored – not totally. Julia seems interested, and Elijah is interested in the way she is interested.

The Feldsteins leave, with Mrs Feldstein writing down a list of sites they have to see in Rome. The language of the restaurant slowly shifts to Italian. As the other patrons arrive, Danny, Elijah and Julia lean into their table to offer critiques.

"What I want to know is this," Julia begins. She has been drinking wine casually and the effect can be heard in her voice. "All of the young Italian men are so gorgeous, right?"

"I hadn't noticed," Danny sniffs.

"Liar!" Elijah cries. "They are absolutely beautiful, and you know it."

"OK," Danny concedes.

"Exactly!" Julia smiles. "They all have this perfect proportion, this delicate balance of divinity and boyishness. I can hardly manage to walk down the street without kissing a dozen strangers. When I'm around them, I feel like such a woman. So my question is this: what happens? You see all of these beautiful young men... and all of the old men are at least two feet shorter, round and balding. There's no trace of the young men in the old men. None whatsoever. It's like they dance at the ball until they're thirty, then – poof! – the midnight bell chimes. They shrink back to size, and their Fiats turn into pumpkins."

"What an awful thing to say!" Danny gasps in his most

scandalized voice.

"But true, eh?"

"Absolutely true."

There is a pause, and then Danny asks, "So what brings you here?" He is still thinking of her walking down crowded narrow alleyways, kissing strangers.

"It's an old story," Julia says, leaning back in her chair. "Only for me, it's new. I went to school for industrial design. All my life, I've been fascinated by chairs – I know it sounds silly, but it's true. Form meets purpose in a chair. My parents thought I was crazy, but somehow I convinced them to pay my way to California. To study furniture design. I was all excited at first. It was totally unlike me to go so far away from home. But I was sick of the cold and sick of the snow. I figured a little sun might change my life. So I headed down to L.A. and roomed with the friend of an ex-girlfriend of my brother's. She was an aspiring radio actress, which meant she was home a lot.

"At first, I loved it. I didn't even let the summer go by. I dove right into my classes. Soon enough, I learned I couldn't just focus on chairs. I had to design spoons and toilet-bowl cleaners and thermostats. The math never bothered me, but the professors did. They could demolish you in a second without giving you a clue of how to rebuild. I spent more and more time in the studio, with other crazed students who guarded their own projects like toy-jealous kids. I started to go for walks. Long walks. I couldn't go home because my roommate was always there. The sun was

138

too much for me, so I'd stay indoors. A certain kind of indoors – the anonymous indoors. I spent hours in supermarkets, walking aisle to aisle, picking up groceries and then putting them back. I went to bowling alleys and pharmacies. I rode in buses that kept their lights on all night. I sat in Laundromats because once upon a time Laundromats made me happy. But now the hum of the machines sounded like life going past.

"Finally, one night I sat too long in the laundry. The woman who folded in the back – Alma – walked over to me and said, 'What are you doing here, girl?' And I knew that there wasn't any answer. There couldn't be any answer. And that's when I knew it was time to go.

"I had saved some money – not much, but enough. I was far from home, and my first decision was that I couldn't go back. I chose Europe because it was somewhere else, and I'd always wanted to go there."

"You thought you'd be happier here," Elijah says.

Julia shakes her head. "Not really. But I figured if I was going to be miserable, I might as well be miserable for different reasons."

"And are you miserable?" Danny asks.

"Strangely, no."

He can't help but look her in the eye and ask more. "And have you found what you're looking for?"

Julia looks at him quietly for a moment, then shrugs. "I don't even know what I'm looking for, although I hope I'll know it if I

139

find it along the way. Sometimes I want to simplify my life into a single bare thing. And other times I want to complicate it so thoroughly that everything I touch will become bound in some way to me. I've become quite aware of my contradictions, but there's no true resolution in that."

The waiter returns, a conversational semicolon. Dessert and coffee are deferred. Danny tries to look Julia in the eye again, but she is studying the tablecloth, finger-tracing lines around the remaining silverware.

Elijah reaches over and touches her hand. He feels nervous and brave. She looks up and doesn't pull away.

Danny takes care of the check.

Outside, night is just beginning. The sun has been down for some time, but the Italians use another definition for night. As Elijah and Danny leave the restaurant, they take turns holding the door for Julia. She murmurs thank you to each and lifts on her toes when her face first touches the night air.

"Now what?" Danny asks.

Elijah is taken aback. He thought it was obvious.

"We're going to go for coffee," he says discreetly.

Danny's energy fades at once, confronted with a "we" that doesn't include him.

"Oh," he says. "Of course." Then, "Do you need money?"

"No. Thank you."

Danny waits for a moment. He wants to see if Julia is going to say anything. If she wants him to stay, he will.

But Julia remains silent, swaying from foot to foot.

Elijah wants to ask his brother what he's going to do, but is afraid it will sound too cruel.

"Don't wake me when you come back," Danny says instead. Then he turns to Julia and tells her it's been nice to meet her.

"Absolutely," she replies. "Thank you for dinner. I'm sure we'll see each other again soon."

"I'm sure."

Danny moves his hand in a little wave and makes his departure. After he's walked a block, he turns around and sees Julia and Elijah in the same lamplight frame, discussing where to go next. Their bodies are not touching, but their expressions are.

Danny turns back to the street and heads for the hotel.

"He seems nice," Julia says, some minutes later.

"Well, I wouldn't call him naughty, if that's the other choice," Elijah replies. They are walking alongside the Arno – the sidewalk is also a river, of men in jackets and women with jewellery headed out into the evening. The last thing Elijah wants to talk about is Danny.

"So the two of you don't get along?"

"Not really."

How many times has Elijah heard this question before? Even though it's a question, it contains the speaker's own observation: *I've seen the two of you and know you don't get along. Isn't that true?* Elijah could say so much more than a simple "not really". He could compile lists of incidents and spites. But then, when he recited them, he would sound bitter and mean – in other words, he would sound just like Danny. One of the worst things about Danny is the tendency to take on Elijah's qualities when talking to or about him. Elijah can hardly bear it. So ignoring it – ignoring *him* – seems like the best idea.

But Julia persists. "Still, he seems to care about you."

Elijah wonders what observation *this* statement could be based upon.

"Not really," he mutters again.

"I think you're wrong."

Elijah is growing impatient – Danny is souring the conversation from afar. "*Look*," he says, and immediately modifies his tone. "I guess you just haven't known us long enough. He doesn't really care about me at all. Not in any way that matters."

"Why do you say that?"

"Here's an example." Elijah stops on a street corner and points to his shoes. "My shoelaces. I know they come untied a lot. I am aware of the situation. But every chance Danny gets, he's telling me to tie my shoes. At least once an hour, sometimes more frequently. And I wouldn't mind it – I swear I wouldn't mind it – if he was actually concerned about my well-being. If he was worried about me tripping into traffic, I would tie them every time. But no. He doesn't care whether or not I fall on my face. He wants me to tie my shoelaces because untied shoelaces *annoy* him. They *embarrass* him. They *get on his nerves*."

"How do you know?"

"Believe me, I know. If you live with someone all your life, you can tell when you are annoying them. Their face just shuts down. Their words sound almost mechanical, because they are reining in all the other emotions. I think I'd also know if I made Danny happy, but I never make him happy. Ever."

Elijah's never said these exact words before, and now that

he's said them, they seem even more real. They are so real, they scare him. Because Elijah fundamentally wants everyone to be happy. With everyone else, he still tries. But he gave up on Danny long ago, for so many reasons that they add up to no clear reason at all.

Julia takes his hand. He thinks the subject is finished, but then she asks, "When did that start?"

She seems so genuinely to want to know the answer that he finds himself talking again. "I guess it was high school," he says.

"So when he was your age now?"

That sounds strange to Elijah, but he guesses it's true. He nods. "About my age. And I was eleven or twelve. Just starting it all, you know. And Danny became a closed door to me. Literally. Wherever he went, the door closed behind him and that's all I'd see. Like I'd done something. When he'd open the door, when we actually saw him, he was always grouping me with my parents, always saying I was taking their side or scamming to get into their good graces. That I was the good son. But the thing is, he'd been good too. Then the doors started closing. And it wasn't even like he was doing anything so crazy. I mean, he wasn't shutting himself in his room and smoking up or looking at porn or sneaking in girlfriends.He wasn't hiding anything but himself. And I just didn't get it."

"Do you get it now?" Julia asks.

"I don't know. I don't have a little brother, I guess. It's

different at my school. I like having the door open."

They have walked past the busier part of town and are now in a streetlight that barely glimmers above the river darkness.

"He's cute, you know," Julia says.

"He is?"

"In that isn't-doing-what-he-wants-to-be way. A look like that, you just want to help."

"In what way?"

"I don't know," Julia says. "You just want to tell him it's OK to be himself."

"And me?" Elijah asks.

Julia arches an eyebrow. "You? You're much easier. You're cute in a cute way."

"Really?"

Julia smiles.

"Really."

Elijah slowly feels lucky again.

Danny has deliberately lost his way. He feels it is too much of a defeat to return to the hotel so early. He is suddenly concerned about what the concierge will think.

So he wanders through Florence, which doesn't feel like Venice at all. He walks down to the Arno, to be by the water. He leans against the railing and stares at the other side, thinking of home. A few minutes later, he is distracted by an eager conversation, spoken in a foreign tongue. Not ten feet from him, a young couple talks in an embrace. (*Young* being seventeen or eighteen... this has become young to Danny, and he hates that.) The boy is not beautiful, merely good-looking, wearing (of all things) a beret. The girl has long hair that shifts every time she laughs. To them, Danny is as real as the river or the city – nice, incidental music behind the conversation. Danny turns away, obtrusive in his own eyes. The couple is taking in all the magic of the moment for themselves. They have left Danny with nothing but scenery and air. And the air is beginning to chill.

Danny moves away from the river, back to the streets. Paying closer attention, he realises the packs that pass him are all American. A succession of American collegians – all having the same conversations ("And so I told her to..." "Are you telling me I should...?" "Get out of here!"). They are all attractive, or trying very hard to be attractive. Danny chuckles at this endless parade of semesters abroad. He doesn't feel at all like one of them. He doesn't have their gall or revelry.

It seems entirely fitting when the fluorescent logo of a 7-Eleven rises before him. Amused, Danny steps in – just to see if a 7-Eleven in Florence is any different from a 7-Eleven in Connecticut or California. Slurpee is spelled the same in any language, and while some of the beverages are different, the beverage cases still mist if he opens the door for too long. Struck by impulse, Danny tracks down the snack cakes. And indeed, there it is: the all-new, cosmetic-free Miss Jane's Homemade Petite Snack Cake – translated into Italian.

Danny reads the name aloud, mispronouncing most of the syllables. He grins and beams – these are words that he wrote at a desk thousands of miles away, not even knowing they'd be translated into a language he'd never spoken. Something that travels so far must be, at the very least, a little important.

There are only three snack cakes left. Danny buys them all – one for his parents, one for his office and one for his own delight. He can't wait to show people. He wishes Elijah were with him. He wishes he were with someone who would understand – not just the seventeen-year-old cashier, looking embarrassed in his maroon, orange and white uniform (such a combination has never before appeared in Italy, especially not in polyester).

Buoyed by his discovery, Danny returns to the hotel. But he's not ready for the night to end – not quite yet. Elijah isn't back, so Danny heads for the bar. Since he thinks there is something disreputable about drinking a bottle of wine alone, he drinks by the glass until the world goes soft. He drinks, even though drinking always makes him remember rather than forget. He tells the bartender about the snack cake. The bartender smiles happily and congratulates him.

Danny is happy in return.

WITH THE RIGHT PERSON, YOU CAN HAVE A LATE-NIGHT CONVERSATION at any time of the day. But it helps to have it late at night.

Elijah and Julia are back in Julia's room, in Julia's *pensione*. Elijah touches the blanket and stares at the pictures on the wall, which he thinks of as hers, even though they are not hers at all. All of her possessions are still in a suitcase.

"I didn't have time to unpack," she explains. "You were here so soon."

"I'm sorry if I disturbed you."

"Don't worry – I was already disturbed."

She takes off her shoes, and he follows suit. Although there are chairs in the room, they are far too rigid for casual conversation. So Elijah and Julia sit on the floor, leaning on the same side of the bed.

"I wish we had candles," Elijah says.

"What if we turn the lights off and leave only the lamp on?"

As Julia rises to get the switch, Elijah closes his eyes. He can feel her moving across the room, he can see the change from light to dark, and then the small step back to light. He can feel her returning to him. Sitting next to him. Breathing softly.

"Relax," she says, and the word itself is relaxing.

Do you wonder?

"Who are you thinking about?" Julia asks quietly.

"Nobody. Just my best friend. Wondering what time it is over there."

"Is he back in Rhode Island?"

"Yes."

"Then the night is just beginning."

Elijah opens his eyes and finds that Julia has closed hers.

Their voices travel at the speed of night.

It TAKES THREE TRIES FOR DANNY TO FIT HIS KEY INTO THE LOCK.

"Elijah?" he asks. But the bed is empty, and the room is alone.

Slowly, Elijah and Julia begin to lose their words. They fall from the conversation one by one, lengthening the pauses, heightening the expectation. Her hand moves from his arm to his cheek. He closes his eyes, and she smiles. He is so serious. The first kiss is clear, ready to be set for memory. The second and the third and the fourth begin to blur – they are no longer singular things, but part of something larger than even their sum.

"Thank you," Elijah whispers in one of the moments of breath.

"You're welcome," Julia replies, and before he can say another word, she kisses him again.

They kiss and touch and trace themselves to sleep. They will wake at sunrise, in each other's arms.

Danny goes to sleep easily, and wakes up two hours later. Nausea infuses every pore of his consciousness. Part of him wants to throw up and get it over with. And part of him remembers what he had for dinner – veal, asparagus, tomato bread soup – and wants to keep it in. Finally, he decides ginger ale is the way to go, and overrules his inner cheapskate to take a swipe at the minibar. Sadly, ginger ale is nowhere to be found. Fanta will have to do.

"Elijah – are you sleeping?" Danny fumbles for the bottle opener and cuts his hand on the cap. He follows the rug to the lip of the bathroom, then liberates four Tylenol from his travel kit. The first Tylenol falls down the drain, but the other three hit their mark, drowned in a tide of too-sweet soda.

Danny still feels sick. But he falls asleep anyway.

IN THE MORNING, THE PHONE WINKS RED AT HIM.

"Meet us at the Uffizi," Elijah's voice says. "We'll see you at eleven."

IT'S JULIA'S DOPE AND ELIJAH'S IDEA TO GO TO THE MUSEUM STONED. Julia rolls him a joint, and then – seeing the happiness in his smile – gives him a little extra to go. After they've smoked, they hold hands through the lobby. The *pensione*'s owner nods a good morning. Julia and Elijah giggle and smile in return. When they reach the door, they break into a skip.

It is eleven fifteen.

Danny waits by the entrance, and then he waits on line. He searches for his brother, and then he gives up. Perhaps Elijah is already inside. Perhaps he won't show at all. Danny is not in the mood for empty minutes. He can barely stand it when he wastes his own time; for someone else to waste it is unconscionable.

The line is very long and very slow. Danny is bracketed by American families – restless children and desperately agreeable parents. The walls of the museum are touched by graffiti: KURT 4-EVA and MARIA DEL MAR 4/4/98 and CLARE 27/03 FRANCESE... TI AMO JUSTIN. One of the American families is accompanied by an abusive tour guide, who takes the children's listlessness to task. "Boredom is a dirty habit," she mutters. The American mother has murder in her eyes.

Five minutes and no Elijah... fifteen minutes and no Elijah... the ticket taker asks Danny to enter, and he does not argue. He decides to start at the beginning of the museum and work his way through history. Elijah will no doubt meet him somewhere in the middle, without realising he's late.

Eᴌɪᴊᴀʜ ɪꜱɴ'ᴛ ꜱᴜʀᴘʀɪꜱᴇᴅ ᴛʜᴀᴛ ʜɪꜱ ʙʀᴏᴛʜᴇʀ ʜᴀꜱɴ'ᴛ ᴡᴀɪᴛᴇᴅ. Rᴇᴀᴌᴌʏ, ɪᴛ doesn't matter. Elijah is happy to be here, is happy to be with Julia. His buzz is just right – enough so things seem real close, but not so much that things seem real far away. He and Julia are surprised by the length of the line; luckily, Elijah strikes up a conversation with the trio of Australian women in front of them, so the time passes quickly. Maura's fortieth birthday is three days away; Judy and Helen are planning to take her to the most expensive restaurant in Siena, bringing at least four bottles of wine. They are legal secretaries – they met in high school and their fates have been tied together ever since. They ask Elijah and Julia how long they've been together, and Elijah revels in the fact that they've seen fit to ask.

"It's been ages," Julia replies, wrapping her arm around Elijah and snuggling close.

"At least three hundred years," Elijah adds.

Once inside the Uffizi, Elijah is dizzied by the ceilings. Julia has to remind him to watch where he steps. A guard looks at him curiously, so Elijah says hello, and the guard suddenly becomes less guarded.

There are so many paintings, all with the same plot. Mary looks stoned, and the Jesus babies are still scary. It's the glummest Sears Family Portrait in history. The angels are all the same person, and the skies are always the same blue.

"Come here," Julia whispers, pulling Elijah to his first Annunciation of the day. "Look closely. I love this scene. Gabriel is telling Mary the story of the rest of her life. Every artist has a different take on it. Like this one."

Elijah leans closer. Indeed, Mary's slight boredom – all too evident in the mother-son shots – has disappeared. In this painting – by someone named Martini – Mary looks uncomfortable. She's not sure about what she's being told. Gabriel, meanwhile, wears a pleading expression. He knows what's at stake.

"Let's see all the Annunciations," Elijah says, a little too eager, a little too loud.

"Absolutely," Julia agrees.

Elijah takes one last look at Mary and Gabriel. Mary winks at him and tells him to move on.

Danny's guidebook talks about Piero della Francesca's "daring search for perspective" – and, quite frankly, Danny doesn't get it. How can you discover perspective? Why did it take thousands of years for artists to discover a third dimension? How can you discover something that is already there?

It's only the fifteenth century and already Danny is getting tired. All these people in robes, with their wooden pastures and wooden expressions. Then the burst of Botticelli. The people are no longer bloodless; Danny can almost believe they have hearts.

"Hey there," someone says. Danny assumes she's talking to someone else. Then he feels a hand on his arm. He turns to find Julia.

"Where's Elijah?" he asks.

"Oh, around. I figured I'd try to find you."

"He didn't want to join you?"

"I don't think he realises I left. He's rather transfixed."

"Good for him."

Julia gestures to the painting, Perugino's *Crucifixion*. "I wonder about the red hat on the ground."

Danny nods. "I was just thinking the same thing."

"I also wonder why they're so clean."

"As opposed to what? A pornographic crucifixion?"

"No. I mean *clean*. Think about it. People in the sixteenth century – not to mention in Jesus's time – didn't look like this: perfect skin, perfect hairdos, spotless clothes. These are people who went to the bathroom in the street, for God's sake. There's no way they looked like this. But that's how we're going to remember them. Our alabaster past. When nothing else is left, art will become the truth of the time. Then people will get to the nineteenth and twentieth centuries and wonder what happened – how we all became so imperfect."

Danny doesn't know what to say to this, and Julia becomes immediately self-conscious.

"Sorry," she says, ducking her head down. "Shove me into shallow water, you know."

"No – you're absolutely right. I've never thought of it that way."

Danny sees that Julia can't decide whether he's being true or whether he's just being kind. It doesn't occur to her that the two can be one and the same.

ELIJAH FIGURES JULIA HAS MADE HER WAY TO THE LADIES' ROOM or something, so he continues on his trail of Annunciations. *Primavera* momentarily gets in the way – Elijah is shocked at how dark it has become. Elijah has always looked to the painting for joy, but now the dark angel in the corner gains prominence. The right-hand maiden is trapped in his grasp. The woman in the centre of it all seems detached, resigned.

Still, people flock to her. Elijah stands in front of the tourist flashbulbs, trying to protect her. A torrent of foreign words tells him to move. But he will not. Each time a camera is raised, he gets in the way. There are signs everywhere saying not to take pictures. And yet everyone acts like he's the one doing something wrong.

Once the latest tour group has passed, Elijah returns to Mary and Gabriel. In Botticelli's version, Mary seems demure, almost faint. Gabriel looks like a woman – perhaps an easier way to convey the news, with a flower held like a pen in his hand. Elijah wishes Julia were around to ask – *How did Gabriel persuade her? Why isn't she frightened by the sight of his wings?* In the frame, Mary sits on the edge of what looks like a tomb. *Isn't she surprised the angel is kneeling at her feet?*

DaVinci's *Annunciation* is almost like a sequel to Botticelli's. Gabriel is in the same pose, but Mary seems to be acknowledging him. She has become regal, undoubting. She is no longer sitting in a room, with the wide world merely alluded to through a window. It is the opposite now. Elijah does not like this Mary. She is too steely, whereas Botticelli's is too weak.

A few galleries later, Elijah gazes again at the ceiling. The details are surreal. A knight stands atop a dragon, about to swing his sword at an armless angel who has breasts, a tail and a mermaid limb that trails off into a small tree.

"Man, that's so messed up," Elijah murmurs.

It's like the ceiling has dredged the dope back into his bloodstream. The paintings are going freaky. Caravaggio's *Medusa* is a scary, screaming bitch.

A very papal-looking portrait watches over *Slaughter of the Innocents*. Elijah can't believe how sexy the slaughter seems. He's strangely turned on. Gentileschi's *Santa Caterina d'Alessandria* holds her breasts in a very provocative way, leading Elijah to wonder what kind of saints they had, way back when.

The rooms are beginning to tip a little. Elijah sits on a bench and stares again at the ceiling. A woman plays violin as a dog and a donkey sit and listen. A man raises a hammer to a bull's head. Three naked women dance, while human heads are superimposed on to the wings of a red butterfly.

"There you are," Julia's voice calls. Elijah is afraid to turn to her, afraid that she too will be written on the wings of an insect, poised to fly away. The dog and the donkey are getting up to leave now. The hammer falls short, and the bull laughs and laughs. Julia sits down next to him and asks if everything is OK.

Elijah closes his eyes and opens them. All the variations go away. Julia is the only real thing he can see.

"I found Danny," she says.

"Good for you. How annoyed is he?"

"Not that annoyed."

"That's probably because I wasn't with you."

Julia sighs. "I told him we'd meet him by Veronese's *Annunciation*."

"So now he's into Annunciations too?"

"No. It was just a place to meet."

Elijah knows he's being a drag. So he concentrates hard to send the bad vibes away. He can feel them disperse, like dark angels dipping away to the sky.

"I'm glad you're back," he says.

They both stand and kiss briefly in front of a small tree that floats on a cloud.

Then Julia pulls away and leads Elijah to his brother.

THE THREE OF THEM STAND IN FRONT OF VERONESE'S *ANNUNCIATION*. Danny doesn't say a word to Elijah about being late. Elijah assumes this is because of Julia's presence.

Mary seems beautifully anguished as a cloud of angels and souls falls on to her. Gabriel is fiercer than before, his finger jabbing upwards, the flowers spilling from his hands.

"I guess you have to feel sorry for her," Elijah says. Julia nods, but she's barely listening. She's still studying the painting, her eyes following the flowers' paths.

"Did Mary have any friends?" Danny asks.

Julia turns to him. "What?"

"I'm the first to admit that I don't know that much about the whole Mary thing. But didn't she have friends? She always seems so alone in these paintings. And then once she has the baby, it's like her previous life never happened."

"I don't know," Julia says. "But it's a good question."

"She probably had friends," Elijah chimes in. "They just didn't want to be in the picture."

Julia has nothing to say to that.

AFTER SKIMMING THE REST OF THE MUSEUM AND DIPPING INTO THE gift shop for a moment (trying to avoid the *Primavera* mouse pad and the *Birth of Venus* outerwear), Julia looks at her watch and makes an announcement.

"I'm afraid I have to leave you for a little bit," she says. "I have plans to meet an old girlfriend for the afternoon." She sees the look on Danny's face and laughs. "Not *that* kind of girlfriend, Danny. Man, you boys are going to need to work on those hang-ups of yours. I'm meeting an old friend from high school who's doing some curating work here. She's going to tell me all about the floods."

Danny is surprised by how sorry he is to see her go. He is not surprised by how sorry Elijah seems. Danny keeps a respectful distance while his brother asks Julia when she'll be back and when they can meet again. Julia touches his cheek and says it won't be long. They make plans for their next encounter.

"So now what?" Elijah asks as Julia heads away. He watches her disappear into the human traffic. He would wave, if only she would see him.

The brothers decide to fall back on tourism, heading to the Duomo and its environs. The austere interior doesn't at

165

all match the delightful exterior, which is itself darkened by car fumes and other modern pollutants. Elijah hangs by the candles, while Danny paces the baptistery and admires the windows.

Elijah cannot believe how tired he feels. It hits him fully, now that Julia is gone. She'd buoyed him into wakefulness. Now he's wrapped in fatigue, all of the sleepless hours catching up to him.

"Maybe we should go back to the hotel? To take a nap?" he suggests.

"Good idea," Danny replies. He too is feeling the full breadth of his tiredness. It's a different tiredness from home – less workmanlike, more atmospheric.

They walk for ten minutes in silence. Then Danny asks, "So what time are you meeting her?"

"About four. You don't mind, do you?"

"Of course not. It's not as if I thought I was going to have dinner with you."

"What do you mean?"

"Nothing. Just a joke. A bad joke."

"Are you sure?"

"Absolutely. I have my book. And I should probably get some sleep tonight."

Elijah can see his brother is bluffing, but he can't think of anything to say besides, "OK."

"Just be ready to leave for Rome tomorrow afternoon."

"OK."

"She seems very nice."

"She *is* very nice."

"I know. That's what I just said."

Back at the hotel, Elijah grabs his toiletry kit and heads straight to the bathroom. Danny realises he's forgotten about lunch. But really, he's not in the mood. Sleep will taste much better.

The water turns on and off. Elijah leaves the bathroom and puts his kit back in his bag.

"What about your girlfriend?" Danny asks.

"Huh?"

"You know. Cal."

"She's not my girlfriend."

"But weren't you going to write to her?"

"I did," Elijah says flatly. But he feels guilty when he says it. It's the truth when measured against the question, but it's hardly the truth when measured against his original intentions. He'd meant to write to Cal every day. He'd meant to live his days as letters to her – turning the trip into a story as he went along. Now the story has become something he can't quite share.

If he sent a letter now, it would get to Providence after his return. The end of the story would precede the beginning. Just the fact that he'll be home in less than a week fills Elijah with dread. He would put off his return for a month, if it meant more time with Julia. He wishes he could conjure a future where Julia came back with him to Providence, and the three of them – Julia, him, Cal – frolicked and conversed for the remainder of the summer. But he knows this can't happen. For a variety of unarticulated reasons.

Danny is already snoring. Elijah looks to his brother and feels a genuine guilt. He hadn't intended to abandon Danny so blatantly. He feels bad about it. But the alternative is to not see Julia at all. And that's impossible.

He hopes Danny will be OK and wonders if there's anything in Danny's life that would help him to understand.

Elijah spots two snack cakes at the foot of Danny's bed. *He just can't escape America, can he?* Carefully, Elijah moves them to the dresser so they won't get stepped on.

He tries to sleep. He closes his eyes and sees ceilings. Melting faces, black woodwork. Saints, inscriptions, murders. Gold, angels, nightmare Popes.

There are good angels and bad angels. There are trees that become clouds.

Julia is gravitating towards him, sliding along in the half of a shell. He is wrestling demons to get to her. Wedding bells ring and children throw crosses in the air.

Only an hour has passed when he wakes up. Danny is still solidly asleep. Quietly, Elijah puts on his shoes and leaves the room. Then he comes back, writes a note thanking Danny for being so cool about everything, and leaves again. He is hours early, but he cannot wait. He will find the bench nearest to Julia's *pensione*.

Then he will wait for her to appear.

Danny is relieved to find it's still daylight. Naps can be devils of disorientation. He is glad to have gotten free before the day has ended. He is not surprised to find that Elijah has gone. But he is surprised by Elijah's note. It's not something Danny would've thought of at seventeen. Danny knows that at that age he would've left without a word.

Part of him can't even believe that Elijah is about to go to college, about to enter that world. Danny still thinks of him as twelve, their parents' favourite, so sure of what is right. But now he's off with a college girl. Or, more accurately, a dropped-out-of-college girl. Something Danny would have only dreamed of when he was seventeen. And maybe still does, from the other end.

Picking up his college copy of A *Room with a View* (never read, alas), he resists the call of CNN and heads to the park square across from the hotel. Most of the benches are already taken. (*Don't these people have jobs?* Danny thinks.) Finally, he finds a spot in the shade. He cracks the paperback spine and settles in. After an hour, he's utterly absorbed and utterly despondent.

Danny puts the book in his lap and searches the park for echoes of Forster. He tries to harken back to a time when being abroad meant something. He searches for a traveller sketching a scene or writing in a journal, as Forster's characters did each afternoon. But instead he sees cell phones and shopping bags, camcorders and an occasional hardcover.

Travel is no longer a pursuit, he thinks. There is something inherently noble about that word – *pursuit*. Life should be a pursuit. But Danny doesn't feel like it is. Or, at the very least, that it's a pursuit of the right things.

The daylight dims, and the people scatter like birds. Danny sits still, watching.

He doesn't know what to do. He heads off to find the statue of David, and figures he'll go from there.

STATUES WAS ONE OF THEIR GAMES. THERE WAS STATUES, AND Runaround, and Penny Flick, and TV Tag. And others now forgotten, invented only for a single afternoon before they disappeared with sundown.

Danny remembers the first time their mother walked in on them playing Statues. They couldn't have surprised her more if they'd been dripping with blood. But instead they were absolutely still, absolutely silent, fully clothed and striking classical poses. A Frisbee for a discus. A Lincoln Log for a javelin. Not looking at each other, because then it would become a staring contest and they would both crack up. So instead they stared into space until a single arm fell or a single leg wobbled.

It couldn't have lasted for longer than a minute. They couldn't have done it that many times. But still, Danny remembers. And when he sees the statues in Florence, he remembers the way he would try to turn himself into carved stone. The way, when Elijah was young, he would secretly be hoping that his younger brother would win. The times he dropped the Frisbee, just to give Elijah that satisfaction. Their mother walking in, not believing her eyes.

In the museum, he tries to mirror one of the statues. He tries to compete again. But it's not the same. He can stare off now for hours. He can avoid moving a muscle. But it doesn't mean anything without someone beside him. It's not a game if he's the only one playing.

Eventually, it's time for dinner. Danny realises he should have given Elijah and Julia the dinner reservations. He is in no mood to eat alone at a fancy restaurant. Nor is he ready to concede a room-service defeat. So he grabs the travel dictionary and heads to a nearby trattoria. Forster keeps him company.

When he returns to the room, nighttime now, he calls the office to check his voice mail. There are no new messages, not even in response to the messages he sent yesterday.

It is a terrible thing to not feel missed.

Danny can no longer read. His head has started to ache again. The Tylenol is no longer in his bag – he must have put it in Elijah's by mistake. In the dim hotel light (why can't hotel rooms ever be well lit?), he opens Elijah's kit and finds a plastic baggie of pot on the top.

"What the—!" Danny cries out, dropping the bag. Then he picks it back up for examination. There's no doubt. Clearly weed.

He cannot believe it. He absolutely cannot believe it. *Elijah is travelling with drugs. He went through customs with drugs. He left drugs in our hotel room. He didn't bother to tell me that we could be arrested at any time.*

It's not the drugs themselves that bother Danny – he's inhaled his share, albeit a while ago. No, it's the stupidity that gets to him. The all-out stupidity of the thing.

Danny imagines the phone call he'd have to make to his parents: *"Thanks for the trip, Mom. But, Dad, we need a little help. You see, we're stuck in jail on a narcotics charge. Do you happen to know any lawyers in Florence?"* Elijah does not care. Everybody thinks he cares. Everybody thinks he's thoughtful. But he's as selfish as anybody else. His kindness has a motive, and kindness with a motive isn't really kindness at all. He pretends to be considerate, and then he leaves his brother to eat alone and sleep alone and pay for every check. He says thank you, but with Danny he never can manage to do something thanksworthy in return.

Why do I bother? Danny wonders. *What holds us together?* Because even though they spent almost every hour of their childhood together, and even though they come from the same town and the same parents, and even though they once genuinely liked each other, Elijah has somehow ended up half a world away from Danny.

"Stupid stupid stupid." Danny puts the drugs back in the kit and the kit back in Elijah's bag. He's not going to risk throwing them out. Just his luck, he'd get nabbed by an undercover *carabiniere* as he left the hotel.

No, Danny has to sit still. He has to wait for Elijah to come home.

And then he will yell.

He hasn't yelled for years. But now he feels like yelling.

Before he can calm down – before he even has time to settle – he hears the key in the door. He stands his full height. He doesn't care how late it is. He doesn't care if Elijah is in some dreamy foreign-girlfriend bliss.

Elijah will have to answer for what he's done.

There is no thank you that can get him out of this.

The door opens.

Danny reaches for the evidence.

But it's not Elijah.

It's Julia.

"Is this a bad time?" she says. "I didn't want to wake you, so I borrowed the key."

She closes the door.

"Where's Elijah?" Danny asks. Has he known somehow to stay away – to stay in the hallway, even?

"Oh, he's asleep. He forgot to take extra clothes, and I was in the mood for a walk. So I decided to come here. You don't mind, do you?"

"No. Sure. Whatever."

It's too late for Danny to tuck in his shirt or to pick up his dirty socks from the floor. Julia doesn't seem to mind. She starts moving for Elijah's bag – Danny stops her.

"Allow me," he says, and puts Elijah's kit on the pillow, taking out the necessary clothes from underneath.

"Thanks." There is a nervous edge to Julia's voice. Danny

wonders if his behaviour has given the whole secret away. Even though he's angry, he doesn't want to get her involved.

"It's really nice of you to come all this way," Danny says awkwardly. "I mean, I'm sure Elijah doesn't mind wearing the same clothes two days in a row..."

"That's not why I came here." Julia has stepped back now. She's looking Danny straight in the eye.

"Oh." Danny is holding out one of Elijah's shirts. He doesn't know what to do with it.

"I came here to see you."

"Oh."

"Which is entirely crazy. So I'll go now."

Flustered, Julia moves to the wrong door and heads straight for the closet. Then, realising her mistake, she doubles back.

"Look," she says, "I don't mean to complicate things. I mean – I know this is complicated. And I'm not sure why I came here. I just wanted to see you and see what happened when I saw you. And now I have, and I've made a complete fool of myself, so I'm going to go, and you can just pretend that it never happened."

Danny puts Elijah's shirt on the bed. He studies this strange girl. And maybe it's because he's angry, or maybe because he's tired, or maybe because he's intrigued – whatever the case, he says, "You haven't made a complete fool of yourself."

"Yes, I have."

"I just don't understand." He wants clarity. He wants to

define the situation. Even as he reads it in her eyes.

"You mean, about Elijah?"

"There's that."

"I don't know. I like him. Really, I do. But today in the museum, I thought that maybe..."

"Maybe?"

"I swore to myself when I came to Italy that I wouldn't let chances go by. You know?"

Danny nods.

"You see," Julia continues, "Elijah doesn't know lonely. You know lonely, and I like that."

She has come a little closer now. Or maybe he's the one who's moved – in all the confusion, it's hard to tell. Danny is undeniably attracted to her. He wouldn't have predicted it, but there it is. She is not his type, but she makes him wonder if he truly knows what his type is. He is conscious of her breathing, and his own. One more step will be too close, and not close enough.

"I was hoping that we could... I mean, I want you," she says.

He is not used to hearing the words. The tone.

It's nice.

You know lonely, and I like that.

He moves away from her to turn off the lights. He wants to see her in shadow. He wants to know what he wants.

There is still light from the street lamps that dangle over the park outside. She is a whisper now, her expression turned entirely to words.

"Come here," she says. It doesn't seem real. His senses are jangling and his temperature is rising and this is a girl he hardly knows, who has appeared as if conjured, bringing everything wrong and everything right.

He doesn't want to mention Elijah's name. Not because he is afraid it will turn her away. No, he is afraid that she will dismiss it, say it doesn't matter. He is afraid he will believe her and of what he will then do.

Elijah.

Alone in a hotel room – a neat role reversal. While Danny is here with his temporary girl and his stupid drugs.

Elijah.

Julia is close enough to kiss. Her scent is all over the moment. Her eyes are watching his. She is as uneasy and vulnerable as he feels.

"Come here," she says again. "It'll be all right."

It would be so easy. To whisper, "I know." To lean into the embrace. To let the lighting dictate the future. To shut off the sense of anywhere but here.

It would be so easy.

And yet Danny turns his head. He breaks the stare. He pushes the moment away.

"What is it?" she asks.

And again, he can't say Elijah's name. Because she will give him a reason to get past it. She will give him the reason to go on.

It would be so easy.

"I can't" is all he says.

She nods. She backs down.

She shivers.

"It was crazy to come here. I'm sorry."

"It's OK."

"No, really."

"Really."

Go back to my brother.

Stay away from my brother.

She gathers herself and leaves the room. The hallway brightness flashes, and then it's dark again.

Come here.

Go away.

Please.

Elijah is an atheist, but he prays. In the quiet, pre-sunlight morning, he is thankful for the path that has led him to this moment, to this bed. He is not thankful to anyone or anything specific. He does not bargain – or even hope – to make the moment longer. He believes in everyday graces. He believes that nothing is arranged, but everything is an arrangement. The angle of Julia's naked shoulder is not preordained. But he is thankful just the same. The lift and release of his breath is not something to be measured. And he is thankful nonetheless.

He will not wake her, and he will not sleep. He will lay in wonder, and he will daydream.

"CAN I COME TO ROME WITH YOU?" SHE ASKS, AS SOON AS SHE opens her eyes.

"Of course," he replies.

Danny is amazed that he's slept. Of all nights to sleep. The emotions that would have singularly kept him up – anger, lust, confusion – combined to exhaust him into submission. Now he's awake, and the evening returns to him like a movie remembered – every word was said, but none of it seems real.

He thinks about home and about going home. Every vacation has a shelf life, and maybe this one will expire before Rome.

He doesn't expect Elijah to come back anytime soon. But, strangely enough, the door opens a little after nine. For an instant, Danny hopes that Julia has returned. He closes his eyes and recognises that the footsteps aren't hers. Elijah is back, packing up.

Danny feigns sleep. Elijah is careful, quiet. Danny knows this could be seen as respectful. But really, Elijah doesn't want to get caught.

Danny waits until Elijah is close by. At the foot of the bed. Hovering over his clothes.

Then Danny opens his eyes and says, "I found your drugs."

Elijah stops what he's doing and turns to his brother. "You found me drugs?"

"No. I found *your* drugs."

"Oh, you mean the pot?" Elijah is rooting through his bag, looking for something. "Feel free to take some."

Danny sits up now. "You're kidding, right?"

"No, really. Go crazy. I think Julia can get us more."

"So they're Julia's drugs?"

"They're not *anybody's* drugs, OK? They're, like, community property."

Elijah is so laid-back – feeling generous, even. Danny wants to strangle him.

"I have just one question," he says. "Do you ever think? For just one moment out of your dippy happy life, do you ever think about things? About little things like international laws, or my feelings, or our parents."

"Our parents aren't little things, Danny."

"DON'T DANNY ME," Danny yells. "We have to talk. Right now. About you. And thinking. Because I don't want some Italian cop pulling us over and busting our asses. And I'm not sure that you should be spending all your time with this Julia."

Now he's got Elijah's attention.

"What do you mean, *this* Julia? Don't drag her into your guilt trip, OK?"

Danny's on his feet now. "I haven't dragged her into anything. You have."

"I have?"

"Yes."

They're facing off now. They haven't done this in so long.

"So what are you saying?" Elijah asks.

"Are you sleeping with her?" Danny asks back.

"WHAT?"

"I said, are you sleeping with her?"

"Are you saying I have to sleep with someone in order to be with them?"

"I'll take that as a 'no'."

"Take what you want. I'm going." Elijah has his notebook now and moves to the door.

Danny blocks him. "Not so fast. I want to talk to you about Julia. I'm just not sure you're seeing everything."

"I thought you liked her."

"I do. I did. It's just that—"

"I'm spending too much time with her. Which means I'm not spending enough time with you. But you know what? I *enjoy* myself when I'm with her. I do *not* enjoy myself when I'm with you. And neither do you. So consider Julia a blessing."

"In disguise."

"What do you mean?"

Danny is so close to telling. He is so close to shattering Elijah into little lovelorn pieces. But he can't. Invoking the moral high ground somehow makes you lose it. Using a secret as a weapon makes you almost as bad as the transgressor.

He will not tell.

Elijah will never know the only good gesture Danny can make.

"Doesn't your wistful romanticism ever get tiring?" Danny sighs.

"No," Elijah says. "*You* get tiring. Look, I'm sorry. But I have to go."

"Where are you going?"

"To Rome. With Julia. We'll take the train."

"Don't be silly."

"I'm not being silly at all. I'm *thinking*, Danny. Isn't that what you want me to do?" In two short minutes, he packs his bag – no hard thing, since he was never around enough to unpack.

"You don't have to do this," Danny says as Elijah reaches the door.

"You don't have to say that," Elijah ricochets. "You don't have to start being nice now. It doesn't suit you. I know where we're staying. I'll see you in Rome."

With that, he leaves.

As he does, Danny realises his shoelaces are untied.

It is too late, though, for Danny to say anything about it. If Elijah trips, there's nothing he can do. If Elijah falls, he will still feel in some way responsible. For having noticed too late.

ROME

As Danny drives the Autostrada del Sole towards Rome, he cannot help but think of everything that's happened. From Julia's hello to Elijah's nonexistent goodbye. The flicker of Julia's glance, the barely bridled fury in Elijah's eyes. For once, Danny wanted Elijah to come right out and say I *hate you*, if only so he could say, Well, I *don't hate you back*.

The cars swerve past him, but this time Danny isn't in a rush. Everything seems so precarious to him. Like driving. Like the fact that all you need to do is move your hand a quarter of an inch and you will be in the next lane. Crashed and dead. So easy.

Concentration. Driving requires concentration, but Danny isn't quite there. He is driving by instinct, like the other thousand strangers upon whom his safety depends. Towns and street signs whiz by, and Danny tries to recall Julia's exact expression. He knows he did the right thing. But still he feels like he's done himself some wrong.

At this very moment, Elijah and Julia are on a train. Or maybe they're still in Florence, dancing along the Ponte Vecchio. Elijah is ignorantly grinning, laughing at the performance. But who is Julia thinking about? That is what Danny wants to know.

He tells himself it's just a summer thing. Fling is such an apt word – it casually throws you. Then life resumes.

Danny drives. He wishes he could tell the truth to someone, so it could be recognised.

"It's good to share a life." His mother had said this to him not too long ago. He had come home for Sunday dinner, something he tried to do once every month. His parents, as always, were on their best behaviour – only minimal discussion of Elijah, and virtually no mention of future weddings or grandchildren. Many of Danny's friends – especially his female friends – faced a terrifying litany every time they stepped into their parents' home: Aren't you getting old? We're not getting any younger. Isn't Alexandra a beautiful name for a baby girl? But Danny's parents were good. Either they had faith that they didn't have to interfere, or they'd already given up hope. The only marriage reference came after dinner while Danny's mother washed and Danny's father dried. They had done this for as long as he could remember, with the radio turned on to the news.

"Don't you ever want to dry?" Danny had asked his mother.

And she'd smiled and said, "It's good to share a life."

Making it sound so easy.

Danny was approaching Rome now. He could see Coca-Cola signs and Mel Gibson billboards. The return of the common culture. Something he could be a part of. Larry King nightly in seventy countries worldwide. Star Wars chat rooms on the

Internet. Madonna in any language. The closeness and the emptiness of it all. And Danny in his Avis rent-a-car, turning on the radio, hoping it will help.

It's good to share a life – and it's good to share minutes and hours too, Danny thinks. With a wife. With a husband. With a boyfriend, girlfriend, best friend. With a fling. With a brother.

For a moment, one brief moment, Elijah and Julia run out of things to say. They are on the train, headed south through Tuscany. They have just been talking about windmills, even though there aren't any windmills in sight. Julia was recalling Amsterdam, and Elijah drew her outward. He asked her about tulips, then asked her about windmills. He himself has never seen one. But they've appeared in his dreams, each a different colour, swirling as they spin.

"Ah, the windmills of your mind," she says. Then falls silent.

He doesn't know what to say next.

She stares out the window – he can see her reflected over the moving countryside. Her eyes aren't fixed on any one place. They are fixed on the blur.

Her expression is the kind that shifts the air into stillness and cold.

"Julia," he says gently, throwing her name into the breach.

It takes her a second to turn. Then she smiles tenderly.

"You have no idea how confused I am," she says.

"So give me an idea."

She just shakes her head.

"I don't want to taint you. I want you to remain clear."

Can't you see you're confusing me already? Elijah wants to say. But he doesn't. He wants to unburden her, not the opposite.

He lets her turn back to the window. He takes out *Pictures from Italy*. As she looks out the glass, she reaches back for his hand. He lets her take it. The book rests against his chest, open and unread.

Elijah feels like a grown-up, with a grown-up love.

Danny gets lost, so incredibly lost on his way into Rome that he almost pulls off to the side of the road and abandons the car. His hotel, d'Inghilterra, must be on some obscure street, since everyone he asks just shrugs or points vaguely. Hemingway once slept there, but that doesn't help.

It's always a low when life begins to imitate an old Chevy Chase movie. He circles the same roads at least ten times, searching for any sort of direction. He vows never to rent a car in a foreign country again. Next time, he'll take the train, or a taxi between cities, if that's what it takes.

Danny curses up a storm. And feels stupid. Because cursing in front of company at least generates an effect. Cursing alone is like taking a Hi-Liter to futility.

At the seventy-eighth red light, Danny leans over and asks directions from a cab driver. The cab driver, amazingly, says, "Follow me." In just two short minutes, Danny is in front of the hotel. He tries to run out and pay the driver, but the taxi is gone before he can even make the gesture.

"Your reservation is for *due*," the stark man behind the reception counter says, his voice carrying through the grand hallway before being absorbed by the curtains.

Danny nods.

"And the other party?"

"Is coming."

"*Oggi*?"

"I believe so."

Danny is perversely afraid that word will get back to his parents: *Your sons didn't check in together. They must have had a fight.*

Danny knows this will be viewed as his failure.

"*What did you do*?" his mother will ask, followed by a dollar-a-minute pause.

"*Nothing*," he'll reply.

And then she'll say, "*That's exactly what I thought.*"

As they pull into the Stazione Termini, Julia turns to Elijah and says, "It's OK. I'm here now."

"But where have you been?" he cannot help but ask.

"It doesn't matter," she replies. Even though it does.

With all due respect to d'Inghilterra, Danny decides he is sick of Italian hotels. There is something to be said for opulent lobbies, but he would trade in every last ornamentation for a well-lit, generously bedded room where the towels are not made of the same material as the tablecloths.

All of the driving has taken its toll, and although Danny refuses to nap, his senses are blunted as he walks outside the hotel. *I am in Rome*, he says to himself, trying to muster the vacation's last waning pulse of enthusiasm. It is too late and too grey to go to the Pantheon – he wants more celestial weather for that. So instead of the Usual Attractions, Danny shifts gears and decides to go shopping. Not for himself. He can't imagine anything more boring than shopping for himself. But his gift list must be reckoned with. He must lay his souvenirs at the altars of his co-workers, lest they think he hasn't been thinking of them while he was away.

The list is still neatly folded into his wallet. Gladner and Gladner. Allison. Perhaps John. Mom and Dad, of course. His assistant, Derek.

Since his hotel is near the Spanish Steps, Danny decides to

duck his head into the posher stores. Especially for Gladner and Gladner. He thinks it would be most appropriate to buy them ties. And maybe a tie for his father.

So he heads to the men's stores and is met with gross indifference. Clearly, a customer is not important unless he or she is Japanese. Danny has never been able to stand disdainful salespeople, but after he storms out of four stores, he realises he must accept his least-favoured-nationality status if he's going to get Gladner and Gladner something classy.

The prices are extraordinarily high. But Danny thinks, *If you're not going to buy an expensive gift for your bosses, then who are you ever going to spend money on?*

He thinks this for a good five minutes as he shuffles through the tie racks. Then he asks himself, *What the hell am I doing?*

Gladner and Gladner already have ties. They have closets full of ties. And most of them are spectacularly dull. Polo stripes and wallpaper prints.

When Gladner and Gladner go away on vacation, they don't bring anything back for Danny. Not even a pen with a floating Eiffel Tower or a paperweight of the Sphinx.

Danny steps away from the tie racks. He steps out of the store. The salesmen do not nod a goodbye. He is not even there to them. He is nobody.

The street is aswarm with people. Danny stands like a hydrant and looks over his list. It is so short, really. Take off Gladner and Gladner, and he is left with five people. Two parents. One co-worker. One assistant. One work-friend.

The question blasts through him. Paralyses him.

How did my world get so small?

A pack of students pushes him aside. Two girls giggle at his slow reaction.

Two parents. One co-worker. One assistant. One work-friend.

This is not my life, he thinks. There are college friends, and Will, and his high school girlfriend Marjorie, who he meets for lunch every now and then.

They're just not on the list.

But they could be.

Danny shoves his hands in his pockets, digging for a pen. He needs a new list.

Allison, yes. Derek. And John, without a question mark this time. And Will. And Marjorie. And Joan and Terry, even though they live in California and the gift will have to be shipped.

No Gladner. No Gladner.

Allison first. Allison, who puts up with him. Allison, who smiles and kvetches and asks him out for a beer, even though he's technically the boss. He wants to buy her something special. Not chocolate – he's always brought her chocolate, even when he went to Houston and other areas not known for their confectionary. No, he wants to find her something that she especially would like. So she can know that he has an inkling of who she is.

Three stores later, he finds it: a hand-sewn journal, its cover a painted river.

And for John, a pair of opera glasses.

And for Derek, a tie more expensive than Gladner's or Gladner's.

And for his mother, a scarf made of seven fabrics, woven with gold threads.

And for his father, an antique deck of cards.

And for Will...

Danny doesn't know.

Is Will the same person now, or would any gift bought for Will be one year, five months and now five days out of date?

Is the Jesus night-light still appropriate? The clapping nun?

The blue-glass lamp that glows rather than burns?

They all seem right, but uncertainly so.

So Danny returns to his room, takes out the hotel stationery and begins to write a very long letter.

MEANWHILE, ELIJAH AND JULIA ARE IN ANOTHER HOTEL ROOM, IN another part of town. Elijah is feeling amorous, but Julia fends him off with her *Let's Go!* guide. Relenting, Elijah says he wants to go stoned to the Vatican. Julia vetoes this idea. Her rebellious streak goes only so far.

"You've offended my inner nun," she says, slipping her wallet into her bag.

"You have an inner nun?"

"Of course. Every girl has one. Some are just louder than others."

Elijah pauses for a moment, packing his backpack. "Even Jewish girls?"

"*Especially* Jewish girls. Thank Julie Andrews for that."

Outside it is a strange combination of hot and cloudy. Taking hold of Elijah's hand, Julia leads the way. She does not slow down to talk or to point out any of the sights (the shop entirely devoted to chess sets, the man who is putting birdseed on his shoulders to attract the pigeons). Elijah can tell she is determined, but he can't say exactly why.

"Hold on." He's trying to slow her down a little. But she

takes it a different way, and holds his hand tighter, pulling him along.

Something has changed between them. The challenge for Elijah is to find out what exactly it is and what it means. They have left the first stage of romance – the rhapsody of *us*. Where everything is *you-me* or *me-you* or a giddily tentative *we*. Now *him* and *her* are asserting themselves, each given a private, pensive depth. Within the rhapsody of *us*, Elijah could think, I *don't really know you, but* I *will*. Now he is not so sure.

But he will not stop trying. She is still here, and that means something. She is still smiling, and he doesn't wish that to be gone.

The Vatican, Elijah has always been told, is the size of Central Park. And the crowds therein, he soon learns, are akin to a free concert on the Great Lawn. Although it's possible he's seen so many people in one place before, he's never seen them levered into an art museum – pushing, wending, photographing, grasping on to children and purses. It is hard to stand still, not to mention contemplate.

The art is overwhelming. It is overload. There is too much of it to be truly breathtaking. Instead, it comes across as bragging. Or perhaps only the non-Catholics feel that way.

It's disorienting. Julia and Elijah try to trace a coherent path, but the building defies them. There are more twists in the halls than there are angels on the ceiling. Packs of foreign-exchange youth and tough gangs of elderly pilgrims block the corridors as they listen to their overenthusiastic guides.

It's only in the Sistine Chapel that the quiet returns. The hushed, respectful movements subdue most of the flashbulbs.

"It's amazing," Julia whispers, and Elijah has to agree. The creation of Adam is surprisingly small – Elijah had always assumed it took up most of the ceiling. But no, there is so much more. It doesn't even stand on its own – it is part of a history, part of a story. The triumph is the space between the fingers: if God exists anywhere, he exists there. That almost-but-not-quite touch.

Elijah and Julia drift slowly through the chapel. And when they are through, they walk backwards and drift through again.

Outside, Elijah debates going into the gift shop. He can hear Cal saying, *"Don't do it, don't give them a penny."* So he saves his postcard money, but doesn't say anything when Julia buys a souvenir book.

"Who knows when I'll be back?" she says.

"Tomorrow?" Elijah offers. "A week from now?"

Julia shakes her head and smiles.

"A month from now?" Elijah pursues.

They are walking through St Peter's Square, which is actually something of a circle. Elijah is not asking the question he wants to ask, but Julia picks up on it anyway.

"I don't know what I'm doing next," she says. "I don't know where I'll be."

"You could stay here."

"I could."

"Or go back to Canada?"

"Not an option."

"California?"

"Ditto."

"How about the East Coast?" Elijah asks, his voice a nervous suitor. "I know this great town in Rhode Island. You'd really like it."

"You're sweet," she says, patting his arm.

And it's funny the way she says it, because he'd always assumed that *sweet* was a good thing.

Now he's not so sure.

It is July twilight by the time Danny finishes his letter to Will. His hand is raw – he is not used to writing like this. Not on such a scale.

He has told Will everything he could think of and, in doing so, told himself many things that he hadn't thought he'd known.

Whenever I am asked about my life, I invariably answer with a reference to work.

At work I feel needed in a way that I've never been needed before.

My parents tricked me into coming to Italy.

I think they are worried about me.

I don't know.

Elijah is somewhere else in the city. Perhaps that's for the best. Perhaps it's enough that one of us is happy. I can give him that much, and not much more.

It's so strange to have words mean exactly what they're supposed to mean. No manipulation, no subtext, no enticement to buy.

Danny puts the letter in an envelope. He puts the envelope in a book. He puts the book in his bag.

Then he looks around the hotel room, his glance settling on the second, still-made bed.

He wonders where Elijah is. And Julia. But more Elijah.

He imagines Elijah as he is back at his boarding school, the centre of his friends' orbit. Always there for a midnight call. Always ready to listen. Voted Most Likely to Succeed – not because he is the most likely to succeed, but because everyone likes him the most.

It is a dangerous thing with brothers, to think that you could be as strong as them, or as wise as them, or as good as them. To believe that you could have been the same person, if only you hadn't gone a different way. To think that your parents raised you the same, and that your genes combined the same, and that the rest of what has happened is all your triumph... or failure.

This is why so many kids want to believe that their siblings are adopted. So that the potential isn't the same. So that you can't look at your brother and say, I *could have been like him, if only I'd tried.*

Danny doesn't want to be as strong as his brother (Elijah is basically a wimp) or as wise as his brother (Danny has no desire to read Kerouac). It is the goodness that grates. Even if it's mostly false (Danny would like to believe, but doesn't really), Elijah has the gift of talking to people, of being liked by people, and Danny can't help but wonder why he didn't turn out the same way.

Restless, he leaves the hotel. The shops are more welcoming now that they're closed. Danny examines the windows of the Via Borgognona and the Via Condotti.

Then he has a leisurely dinner; he is getting used to eating alone in public. He watches the people at the other tables and drinks plenty of wine.

After dinner is over, he wanders farther. He keeps expecting to bump into Elijah and Julia. Instead, he comes to Trevi – the fountain of youths. Teenagers from various nations are perched around its rim, cackling and flirting and preening. It is a point of convergence for those who are not wearied by midnight and everything after.

Danny stands to the side and watches the swagger, banter and anguish. The packs of girls and the packs of boys collide and separate at will. For Danny, it is like visiting a neighbourhood where he once lived. The familiarity and the distance of it.

He is no longer young, and he is far from old.

They laugh so hard around the fountain. He misses that acutely. Not the folly of entanglements or the drama of indecision. But the laughter. The bold bravado that can take you through the night.

Danny doesn't want to be them, and he doesn't even want to stay and watch them. He only wants to find an intensity to match their own.

Eᴌɪᴊᴀʜ ᴀɴᴅ Jᴜʟɪᴀ ɢᴏ ᴛᴏ ᴀ Fʀᴇɴᴄʜ ᴍᴏᴠɪᴇ ᴡɪᴛʜ Iᴛᴀʟɪᴀɴ ꜱᴜʙᴛɪᴛʟᴇꜱ. Then, as the languages intermingle in their memory, they return to the hotel.

That night, the rhapsody of us returns, in physical form. They have a conversation of movements, silent from the moment they walk in the door. They undress each other completely – tracing, gliding, holding. Only the bodies whisper. Breath signals. Fingers entwine.

It is almost like floating. It is that simple, that understood.

Elijah closes his eyes. Julia kisses his eyelids. He flutters them open, and Julia whispers *"no"*. So he closes them again, and the moment continues.

Elijah feels colours, and wonders if he's in love.

THE NEXT DAY IS JULY 4TH. DANNY WEARS A RED AND WHITE POLO shirt and a pair of blue shorts. He can't help himself.

In the morning, he heads to the ruins. He thinks he will beat the midday heat, but in this he is wrong. The day is scorching, the lack of shade relentless. Danny loses interest quickly. The area he sees, with its rows and rows of broken columns, must have once been grand. But now it is only rows and rows of broken columns. They are not even beautiful. They are merely, admirably, old. Danny takes a few photos, but it's more for historical reasons than out of any visual pleasure.

It is soon unbearably hot. Danny throngs to a streetside vendor in search of Evian. The line is long, but Danny doesn't see he has a choice. As he waits, a hand taps him on the shoulder.

"Danny Silver?" a voice asks.

Startled, Danny turns – and is even more startled to see Ari Rubin, from Camp Wahnkeemakah.

"Ari?"

It must be – what – seven years? More?

"So it *is* you. That's unbelievable."

Ari looks amazing. Tan, tall, his hair no longer in a bowl cut. From Camp Wahnkeemakah. Ages ago.

He doesn't look at all the same. Except it's recognisably him.

"What are you doing here?" Ari asks.

"Vacation," Danny replies, still stunned. Ari was his best friend for three straight summers. They were pen pals for two summers after that, and then drifted apart.

Seven years? More like ten.

Danny has to turn away to buy his bottles of water. But when he turns back, Ari is still there, beaming.

"And what are you doing here?" Danny asks.

"Working."

"Business?"

"Pilot."

Danny laughs. Of course Ari is a pilot. Ari, whose mother would send him a new model airplane every week. Ari, whose bunk smelled like Krazy Glue and balsa wood.

A pilot.

"I can't believe I recognised you."

"Me neither."

They lost touch because Danny lived in New Jersey and Ari lived in Ohio, and neither of them liked to talk on the phone. But when they'd been at camp, they were nearly inseparable. They planned all their activities together, requested the same bunks, and even tried to be on the same Colour War teams. There was one time, the second summer, when Danny had been stuck in the infirmary with a flu bug. The only thing to do in the infirmary was watch videos. Which would have been an unparalleled delight, except the only two movies they had were *Annie* and *Predator*. Danny would have gone absolutely bonkers if Ari hadn't come to his window at every available break, telling him what was going on and making jokes to count away the hours.

Danny can see that Ari is as amazed by this surreal reunion as he is. They lost touch because of the distance between New Jersey and Ohio. Now they meet up in Rome. Of course.

Ari seems genuinely thrilled, but there's also a flicker of worry, a consciousness of time in his eyes.

"You have to be somewhere?" Danny guesses.

Ari nods.

"Now?"

"Yes – but... are you free tonight?"

"Absolutely."

Dinner arrangements are made. Danny cannot stop shaking his head at the coincidence of it all. Ari says goodbye, and as he leaves Danny can see that he's shaking his head too.

Still smiling, Danny heads to the old Jewish ghetto. For at least another fifteen minutes, he doesn't even think about the heat.

Eᴌɪᴊᴀʜ ᴀᴡᴀᴋᴇɴꜱ ᴛᴏ ᴛʜᴇ ꜱᴏᴜɴᴅ ᴏꜰ ʀᴀɪɴ. Oʀ ᴀᴛ ʟᴇᴀꜱᴛ ʜᴇ ᴛʜɪɴᴋꜱ ɪᴛ'ꜱ rain. It's really the hotel's ancient air conditioner, struggling unsuccessfully against the heat of the day.

Julia is nowhere to be found. It is eleven o'clock in the morning, which means Elijah slept for at least four hours. The bathroom door is open and all the fixtures are silent – Julia is not in there, either. Elijah rolls over and throws on some clothes. After a few minutes of vague worry, he hears the key in the door. Julia walks in.

"Where have you been?" he asks.

"Thinking," she replies, and it is to Elijah's credit that he realises: *to Julia, thinking is indeed a place*.

He remembers that it's July 4th, but that seems like a rude thing to mention to a Canadian. So instead he wishes her a very happy Friday, and she in turn looks at him with an almost resigned curiosity.

"Let's go to the Colosseum," she says, and indeed they do. Strangely enough, it is not as intact as Elijah had thought it would be. He'd imagined a full and complex building with part of the rim chipped off. But instead it looks like something unearthed from the Planet of the Apes.

"People died here," Julia whispers.

Elijah pulls her into the shade and begins to kiss her. Almost immediately, he sees he's done the wrong thing. Although Julia's body doesn't move away, it feels as if she's left it. Elijah says, "Well, then," and the two of them move on.

They walk through the ancient city without really saying a word. Elijah wants to go to the Pantheon, but that's where Julia went while he slept. So instead they head to the Piazza Navona, in the hope of sitting down to eat. In the hope of conversation.

Elijah can see that Julia is troubled, and it is the core of his nature to want to make it better. Whenever he says "I'm sorry", she tells him it is not his fault. He knows this. But he is sorry just the same.

He blames time, for there are only two days left until he must return to America. Two days left to answer the question: *And now what?*

The two of them sit on a bench. Julia leans her body into his and closes her eyes. He takes this as a good sign. Although it is wretchedly hot, the sun feels good as it shines across his face. Careful not to shift away from Julia, Elijah studies his surroundings. The fountain at the heart of the piazza is beautiful, topped by an obelisk inscribed in languages from a different time. A blond boy with a pink teddy bear – he must be about six – points at an overweight couple sitting on slim cafe chairs.

There is a breeze. It is nice. A group of fifty or so young Italian women passes by, trailing talk. Another boy chases pigeons. He is running in circles. Elijah closes his eyes and stays still. He and Julia are picture-perfect statues. The fountain splashes in murmurs. The breeze continues. The tourists fade away. A clock that no longer works watches over them.

Minutes pass. Elijah opens his eyes as a bride walks by. Her long gown glides across the stone, picking up the dust of the square. She smiles at Elijah smiling. Or perhaps she doesn't see Elijah at all.

A photographer arranges the full wedding party in front of the fountain – bride, groom and an assemblage of family members, each with a paper fan to rustle away the heat.

Julia pulls away from Elijah and stands. She stares for a moment at the bride and the groom. The expression on her face is a different language to Elijah. And he cannot ask for a translation, for fear of exposing an ignorance that love can't conquer.

Love?

Julia is walking, then waiting for Elijah to follow.

"Julia," he says. But she is already too far away.

THE JEWISH GHETTO MAKES DANNY FEEL HOPE AND SADNESS. HOPE because the Sinagoga Ashkenazita is still there. Sadness because it must be guarded by *carabinieri* armed with machine guns.

After a tour of the Jewish Museum, Danny heads to the Piazza Navona. He has heard that the fountain is beautiful, and it does not disappoint. A wedding party is having its picture taken in front of the obelisk. From the ragged state of their smiles, Danny can tell they've been at it for a little while. The photographer is manipulating the group into preposterous poses, using a lamppost as a prop. The groom lovingly arranges the bride's dress so that she may sit. In this heat, the bride is no doubt wishing she'd worn a miniskirt. The groom is clearly itching to take off his jacket and dive into the water.

Tourists take pictures of the photographer taking pictures.

Danny sits on a bench and watches. In a nearby cafe, a lunchtime guitarist is singing "Knockin' on Heaven's Door", only the refrain sounds much more like "Knock, knock, knockin' on lemon's door".

Soon the song turns to another song. And another. Danny sits and listens and watches as the people pass by.

At long last, the wedding photographs are done. Joy returns to the faces of the bride and the groom. He lifts her up and swings her through the air. The photographer fumbles for his camera, but he is too late. As the bride and groom parade back through the square, the bride looks at Danny and gives a little smile and salute. Danny smiles back, and wonders where such familiarity came from.

"LET'S GET DRESSED UP FOR DINNER," JULIA SAYS. IT IS THE END OF the day – all the ruins have been visited, all the squares have been crossed. Elijah is exhausted.

"I'm not sure I have anything to wear," he confesses.

"Didn't you bring a suit?"

"I'm not sure I own a suit."

"I'll bet Danny brought a suit."

"I'll bet Danny couldn't travel without one. Just in case there was, you know, a business emergency."

Julia pulls a sleeveless black dress from her bag.

"Do you have anything that would remotely go with this?"

"What's the occasion?"

"Isn't it your Independence Day? Or maybe I just want to take you out to a wonderful dinner. Do you think you could deal with that?"

"I think I could manage."

Elijah triumphantly pulls a tie from the bottom of his bag. Julia applauds and slips off her clothes. Before Elijah can react, she is putting on the dress.

She looks even more beautiful with it on.

Danny is nervous that Ari won't show up. He has been looking forward to this too much – he is relying too heavily on a random encounter. He paces the sidewalk in front of the restaurant for twenty minutes – fifteen minutes before Ari is supposed to show and five minutes after. Danny is worried that he misheard the directions. He is worried he is waiting at the wrong place, for the wrong person.

Then Ari appears, apologising the five minutes away. He shakes Danny's hand and ushers him in the door. The maitre d' seems to know him, and the table they get has a spectacular view of the nighttime alleyways.

"I'm so glad I found you," Ari says, sitting down.

"Likewise."

It has been so many years, but they plunge into them quickly. Danny says he can't believe Ari is already a pilot, and Ari tells him how it came to be. He dropped out of Harvard for flight school, which caused his parents no end of grief.

"Is your mom still in Ohio?" Danny asks.

Ari nods. "Same house. Same life. Her gallery keeps getting

bigger and bigger – she just bought out the jeweller next door, so she can expand again."

"And your father?"

"What wife was he on when we last wrote to each other?"

"The second, I think. No wait – he was just starting with... Laureen."

"I can't believe you remember her name!" Ari exclaims. (Neither can Danny, for that matter.) "She actually never made it to the altar. Dad left her for Gail. Now he's with Wanda, soon to be wife number four."

"Do you like her?"

"I like that she's his age."

"Does your mom still make those raisin cookies?"

"Yup. You are still, to this day, the only person who liked them without raisins."

"I didn't appreciate raisins back then."

"You always wanted chocolate chips."

The waiter makes a third pass at the table, and Danny and Ari finally take up their menus. Danny steals glances at Ari as Ari carefully reads the selections. He wasn't a particularly attractive kid, but he's grown up to be an attractive man. Not that Danny can really tell. But he takes some satisfaction that it's not only the bastards who get good looks. Danny remembers back when they were in camp – every body change seemed like an event, shocking and fascinating, the prelude to such alien phenomena as sex and shaving. Now they've crossed over to that other world.

They are comfortable within their own skin (or at least Ari seems to be).

Did they even think about the real future back then? Did they just assume they'd be friends forever?

Danny cannot remember what his younger self foretold.

JULIA TAKES ELIJAH TO A ROOM LIT ONLY BY CANDLES. THERE ARE OTHER people within it, but they are only flickers in the background, sounds in the air.

"This is wonderful," Elijah says. He had tried to stop at an ATM on the way, but Julia wouldn't let him. "It's my night," she had said.

The owner gave Elijah a jacket at the door. Julia said it made him look dashing. Like a film star.

Now she watches intently as he unfolds his napkin and places it on his lap. She is taking him all in.

He picks up the menu, but she waves him down.

"Allow me," she says.

The waiter approaches. His hair is the colour of burnt embers. Julia orders for them both, her Italian faltering in parts.

The waiter nods, understanding. Two minutes later, he is back with the wine, which Julia sips to her satisfaction. The room is warm, and Elijah can feel himself settling into the candlelight glow. The waiter pours the wine. Julia smiles secretly.

"A toast," she says, raising her glass. "To the end."

"I WAS ENGAGED ONCE," ARI TELLS DANNY. "I REALLY THOUGHT SHE was the one. I really thought, *This is it*. I met her while I was in school – we volunteered at the same shelter. Perfect, right? She was a nurse, so that made scheduling a little hard. But we managed. For three years, we managed. I proposed to her the first time she flew with me. My instructor lent me his Cessna. At first, Anna was really nervous – she wasn't a big fan of flying. But I asked her to trust me, and she did. I took her up over the Rockies – it was a gorgeous day, you could see everything. When we hit ten thousand feet, I put on the autopilot, pulled the ring from my pocket, leaned over to her, and asked her to marry me. Right away, she said yes.

"I thought that was the hard part, but I was wrong. We moved in together, which was great when we were both there, but we weren't both there a lot. I graduated, and Continental picked me up. Denver was still my home base, but I had to go wherever they wanted me to go. At first, Anna understood this. She supported it. But after a while it wore us both down. Finally, one night I came home – it must have been two in the morning – and she said it was too much. She said she wasn't sure she was old enough to be anybody's wife. And she sure as hell wasn't old enough to be a pilot's wife. I couldn't argue with her. We both realised we'd gotten as far as we could go, and that the only way to go from there was backwards. And neither of us wanted to go through that."

Ari pauses and takes another sip of his water. "How about you? Anything like that?"

Danny shakes his head. "Nothing."

"Not even a little?"

"Not even a little."

At first, Elijah thinks he's misunderstood her. Or that she's misunderstood him.

"To the end?" he asks.

"To the end," she repeats, taking a sip of wine.

"But tomorrow's my last night. I leave Sunday."

"I know."

He still doesn't get it.

"So why is this the end?"

Julia puts down her glass and says, simply, "Because it is."

Danny is amazed that he feels so comfortable. He is amazed that while there are some people you can see every day and not say a word to, there are other people whom you can see once a year – or once a decade, or once a life – and say anything.

"How's your brother?" Ari asks. "God, he must be old now, right? I remember you writing to me about how you were going to teach him multiplication, even though he was only four. You were going to make him the smartest kid in his nursery school class."

Danny starts off by saying Elijah's fine. Then he finds himself telling Ari everything that's happened – from the moment he got his parents' call to the moment Elijah left the hotel room in Florence. He remembers that Ari has two brothers of his own – two brothers and three stepsisters.

Ari listens carefully. Danny isn't just talking to say things aloud. He is talking directly to him.

"I don't know how we got this way, Ari. I don't know when I stopped wanting to help him, or even when I stopped wanting him to be smart. I *dreaded* coming here with him. I really didn't want him to come – I figured I'd be happier alone. And I don't know whether it's because he was here and then he left, or whether I was just wrong in the first place, but right now I wish he was here. Not at this table with us. But I just wish I knew where he was."

"It's hard."

"Yeah, it's hard."

Ari puts down his fork and looks right into Danny's eyes. "Brothers are not like sisters," he says. From his tone, Danny can tell this is something he's learned. "They don't call each other every week. They don't have secret worlds to share. Can you think of two brothers who are really, inseparably close? No, for brothers it's a different set of rules. Like it or not, we're held to the bare minimum. Will you be there for him if he needs you? Of course. Should you love him without question? Absolutely. But those are the easy things. Do you make him a large part of your life, an equal to a wife or a best friend? At the beginning, when you're kids, the answer is often yes. But when you get to high school, or older? Do you tell him everything? Do you let him know who you really are? The answer is usually no. Because all these other things get in the way. Girlfriends. Rebellion. Work."

"So this is normal?" Danny asks.

"Don't go for normal," Ari suggests. "Go for happy. Go for what you want it to be instead of settling for what it is."

ELIJAH DOESN'T SEE HOW HE AND JULIA CAN GO ON WITH THE MEAL, but they do. She asks him about home, and he finds himself telling her about the time Mindy got fired from her temp job at the Gap because she couldn't fold properly, and the time his friends Max and Cindy got caught making out in Cindy's parents' bed. Her parents never said a word about it, but her mother threw out the sheets.

Julia is laughing and Elijah is smiling, and to any other person in the room they must look like a happy couple. But all Elijah can think is, *It's over*. And there's nothing in Julia's face that says anything different.

"What do you want?" Julia asks over dessert.

"From what?" Elijah asks.

"From love. I mean, from the person you're with."

"Love is enough," Elijah answers.

Julia shakes her head. "It's more complicated than that. I know I'm only, what, three years older than you? But let me tell you, it can get so complicated. Try to keep it simple. Here's what I think. We all want someone to build a fort with. We want somebody to swap crayons with and play hide-and-seek with

227

and live out imaginary stories with. We start out getting that from our family. Then we get it from our friends. And then, for whatever reasons, we get it into our heads that we need to get that feeling – that *intimacy* – from a single someone else. We call that growing up. But really, when you take sex out of it, what we want is a companion. And we make that so damn hard to find."

When dessert is over, Julia pays with a Gold Card. Then she touches Elijah's hand and tells him it's probably time to get his things.

She seems sad when she says it. But he can tell he's not going to change her mind.

Ari walks Danny back to the hotel. He has an early flight the next morning, otherwise they'd probably walk all night. They are talking tangents now, but somehow the tangents connect. Ari is talking about all the places he's been. Danny feels like they are all the places he wants to go. The Sahara. Budapest. Sydney. New York.

Danny pulls Ari into a 7-Eleven and shows him the Italian translation of his work. Ari is amused, and asks if the snack cake is suitable for framing. Danny says he doesn't think so – but perhaps that can be the slogan for the new Pop-Tarts campaign.

Ari wants to buy one of the Divines, but Danny is afraid he might actually try to eat it. So instead they get Slurpees – their own shamelessly American way of celebrating the Fourth of July.

"So your job sounds like fun," Ari says as they leave the convenience store.

Danny nods. "I'm afraid that's the problem. Maybe I enjoy it too much."

"I know what you mean."

"Someday we'll have a balance, right?"

"Someday. Yes."

Across Rome, towers chime midnight. Danny raises his Slurpee in a toast.

"To reunions," he says.

"To reunions," Ari echoes.

The Slurpees don't taste the same as they used to. Maybe that's because it's a foreign country. Maybe it's because nothing ever tastes the same as it did when you were ten. Or maybe the 7-Eleven syrup has changed.

Danny and Ari ponder this and soon ponder other things. Before they forget, they exchange addresses and phone numbers and e-mail addreses. Danny promises they will keep in touch.

At the hotel, Ari hugs Danny goodbye. Danny is not used to being fully hugged – just the sports-guy hugging-without-touching. But this is the real thing, the hug that lets you feel held.

They say goodbye at least five times, and then Ari leaves. Danny heads straight back to his room – he's had a wonderful night, and he doesn't want to press his luck. He sticks his tongue out at himself in the mirror and finds that it is still the colour of a neon sky. He remembers how he and Elijah would have contests to see whose tongue could stay blue the longest. Hours without drinking, trying not to swallow needlessly. This makes him smile now. He realises it will always make him smile, if he can hold on to his brother in some way. If he can make his way through all the distractions, back to what they once shared. And still share.

He takes a shower and heads to bed, ready for a good night's sleep. Then, at the last minute, he thinks of something else to do.

He reopens his letter to Will and adds another page.

He writes about how things have changed and how things don't have to change. He can't go back to the past, he knows. But maybe there's a chance of getting Elijah back.

Eᴌɪᴊᴀʜ's ᴘᴏssᴇssɪᴏɴs ʜᴀᴠᴇɴ'ᴛ ʙᴇᴇɴ sᴄᴀᴛᴛᴇʀᴇᴅ ғᴀʀ, sᴏ ɪᴛ ᴅᴏᴇsɴ'ᴛ take him long to gather them. Julia keeps asking him if he's sure he knows where Danny is staying. She offers to call, to let Danny know Elijah is coming. Elijah tells her not to bother.

She won't give him an explanation about what's happening and why he has to leave. All at once, he's realising she's not the kind of person who gives explanations. She might not know herself.

He wants to ask, *Are you sure?* But he's afraid the line between a yes and a no would be frustratingly unclear.

Soon his bag is packed. There's nothing else to do. The maid has already cleaned up. There's just the matter of leaving.

"So goodbye, I guess."

Julia hands him a slip of paper.

"My parents' address," she says. "You can always reach me there."

"Oh."

"Look, I know this probably isn't what you thought would—"

"It's OK. Really. I just have to go."

232

Julia hovers in front of the door. "I mean, when I said it was the end, it wasn't – oh, I don't know. The end doesn't have to be the end, you know. You can stay, if you'd like."

"No. It's OK."

"I see. No, you're right. Can I get your address?"

Elijah writes it down for her. It feels like an empty gesture now, whereas once he thought it would be the key to their future.

"I'm sorry," she says. She hasn't opened the door, but she's no longer standing in front of it. "Tell Danny I'm sorry too."

"For what?"

"For ruining your holiday."

Elijah knows that any goodbye kiss won't end up being a goodbye kiss. So he just bows his head a little and thanks her for dinner. Then he opens the door and leaves. In the hallway, he stops for a moment and waits to hear her turn the lock.

She doesn't, but he heads to the street anyway.

Eᴸɪᴊᴀʜ ɴᴇᴇᴅꜱ ᴛᴏ ᴡᴀʟᴋ. Hᴇ ɴᴇᴇᴅꜱ ᴛᴏ ꜰᴏʀɢᴇᴛ ᴀʙᴏᴜᴛ ᴅᴇꜱᴛɪɴᴀᴛɪᴏɴꜱ and meanings and plans. He feels like a door has opened and he has walked into a world filled with his own mistakes.

Once, when he and his friend Jared were on acid, they stumbled across a pad of Post-its. Immediately, they began to label everything they encountered: DOOR and BOOK and HAND. Each Post-it bestowed a cosmic sense of clarity. The door was a door because the writing said DOOR. The floor was a hand because the writing said HAND. It seemed, for a moment, that they could live their lives that way, as omniscient identifiers and casual illusionists.

Elijah wishes he had the acid now, and the Post-its, so he could make Julia the JULIA he wanted her to be, and his life the LIFE that he had thought he had been living. He wants to bend time backwards so he could write dozens of postcards to Cal, so he could label as SORRY the very things he's now done. If Danny's Post-it said BROTHER instead of DANNY, would that work? Could Elijah take an eraser to ROME and suddenly make it HOME?

He is not angry with Julia. He is confused by her actions, and his own. As he walks through the midnight streets, he tries to reach into her side of the conversation, to pull out the cardinal truths.

He keeps picturing Cal in Providence, walking to the P.O. box, hoping for some word from him.

He imagines them building forts.

He thinks of his parents, and how concerned they'd be to see him walking where all the stores have long since closed.

He imagines Julia back in her hotel room, sitting absolutely still, or moving completely on.

There can be no destination. He can't go back to her, and he can't go on to Danny. He doesn't want to have to account for himself right now. Either Danny will say something and Elijah will explode, or Danny will say nothing and Elijah will disappear completely.

It's not about the city, it's about the walking. Really, he could be anywhere now, because he wants to be nowhere. Rome is lost on him. It's the time of night when no one walks alone. Couples eye him warily, as he walks with his bag slung over his shoulder. He finds himself on the same street he and Julia took to the Colosseum, only it's totally different now.

Every ounce of his soul tells him this will make a good story to tell his friends – an anecdote in the biography, an incident in the life. But part of the sorrow he feels – and it is that – comes from the distance he sees between himself and the storytelling, the hole that has ripped open between the here and the there. He hasn't been thinking of there nearly enough. He hasn't been a good enough friend.

I'm sorry, he says to Cal, and to his parents, and to Julia, and to Danny.

Because he doesn't know what else to say.

"*Stai bene?*" a voice asks.

He has been standing still on the sidewalk. Now he looks across the street and sees a young woman and her date. The man wants to keep walking, but the woman has stopped.

"I don't understand," Elijah explains.

"Are you all right?"

"Oh, yes. Thank you."

"Are you lost?"

"I'm not sure."

"Where are you going?"

"The Pantheon?" Elijah says. It's the first building that comes to mind. "I'm supposed to meet someone outside the Pantheon."

The man laughs and takes hold of the woman's elbow. She shrugs him off, whispering, "*Un attimo.*" Then she crosses the street, pulling a pen from her pocketbook. Her mouth is all lipstick, her eyes dark as the lashes.

"Give me your hand," she says. Elijah holds out his palm. She takes hold of it and draws a map. At the end of the map is a star.

"That," she says, "is the Pantheon."

"*Sofia!*" the man calls. With a curious smile, she turns and runs back across the street.

"Thank you!" Elijah shouts.

"*Avanti diritto!*" she calls back, and is gone.

Elijah stares at his hand. It is a complex map, without any names. Just a beginning, an ending and a path.

Remarkably, he finds his way. Never once closing his fingers. Never once looking anywhere but where he is.

By the time he reaches the Pantheon, there are hints that the sun will soon rise. He sits on a bench and stares at the building's exterior – rather plain, with only a hint of what's inside.

As he waits for it to open, he falls asleep.

Danny arrives first. Elijah arrives second. This time they are separated by minutes, not years.

The Pantheon is empty.

Danny does not notice. He is staring up into the eye of the sky. He is standing in the golden beam of light that falls to the floor. The lifting dome, a chorus of geometry. Crowned by the circle of air, the eclipse of architecture. An opening where nobody would ever imagine one to be.

Elijah wakes up on the bench, gathers himself together, and walks inside. At first he is overwhelmed by the building. The silence. Then he sees the one figure standing there. And knows immediately who it is.

He walks over, puts a hand on his brother's shoulder. Danny turns, and Elijah is moved by the relief that rises to his face. Danny is about to say something, but Elijah gestures him to be quiet.

The two of them look around.

No one but the statues.

Nothing but the space.

They cannot believe it. They marvel at the emptiness. As if

the building has been waiting for them, preparing for this moment and this moment only.

The guard stands by the door, unaware.

The sunlight streams down on them as they look up and ponder the tiles that reach towards blue. The quiet is extra-ordinary.

Elijah walks into the shadows, his footsteps keeping time over marble. Danny begins to circle too, until suddenly they are in orbit around each other, reverently floating through the room. They look at statues and cornices and old-spoken words. They look at the colours that fall under their feet – white marble, red marble, black marble. They look at the dome and the intimation of air. They wait for someone else to walk in the door, but no one does.

They look at each other and share a smile of disbelief and wonder. Their orbit becomes more pronounced, and now they are truly circling each other, not speaking a word, not daring to look away. It is like a dance, because they are partners. It is like a dream, because there is nothing else.

They will have this.

Danny stands in the centre of the light, so the sun can stare down at him. Then he closes his eyes and extends his arms. He can feel the space of the building, like he can feel the building itself beneath his feet.

Elijah stays in the shadows. He too closes his eyes. He holds them closed for a minute, maybe two. For he knows that when he opens them, things will not be as they once were. Tourists will arrive. A cloud will cross the eye. They will no longer be alone together. But they will still be together.

Slowly Elijah opens his eyes and walks to his brother. He thinks of the Statues game. He thinks of red twine spinning from trees, and his brother's hands as they pushed him on the swing.

Elijah extends his arms so that his fingertips touch his brother's. Then, just once, they spin like children.

This is what is lost.

This is what is never lost.

"Where have you been?" Danny asks. His tone is not accusatory; it is genuinely concerned. They are standing in the undirected light of day now, next to a postcard vendor outside the Pantheon.

"Just around," Elijah replies. He knows he must look like a total unbathed freak.

"Where's Julia?"

"In her hotel room, I think. Back there, in the Pantheon, did you...?"

Danny nods.

"So it wasn't just me?"

"No. It wasn't just you. It was just us."

"Wow."

The pleasure on Danny's face flickers. "Are you going back to Julia's now?" he asks.

"No," Elijah says. "We, um, said goodbye."

This is not what Danny was expecting to hear. "Oh," he says. "For good?"

"For good."

Elijah is surprised by how angry he doesn't sound.

241

Danny wants to hear more of the story, but he doesn't really have the grounds to ask. He's never asked before, so it would seem strange to ask now. He also wants to know whether or not Elijah found out about Julia's late-night visit. Elijah doesn't look as if he's found out, but maybe he's just hiding it.

In the end, Elijah will never know, and Danny will never know whether or not Elijah knows.

"So where have you been?" Danny asks. "Where do you want to go now?"

"How about the ruins?"

"Sure."

"You haven't been there already?"

"Nope," Danny lies. (Elijah won't know this is a lie until a month later, when Danny drives up to Providence and brings along his few vacation photos.)

They both take a minute before leaving the Pantheon's sight. Elijah buys a few postcards. Danny takes out a pen, and they write to their parents, thanking them. Then Danny gets out his camera, and they ask the postcard vendor to take their picture. Just to prove they've been here. Together.

As they head off to the ruins, Danny asks Elijah what he's written on his hand.

And Elijah tells him a true story.

WHEN THEY GET TO THE RUINS, IT BEGINS TO RAIN. NEITHER DANNY nor Elijah has an umbrella, and neither will admit he wants one. So instead they dart from overhang to overhang – and end up standing without cover, daring to be drenched.

Elijah is inexplicably moved by the broken columns and fragmented floors. He cannot help but find a meaning and a message in their poverty of stature. *This is what remains*, he thinks. It seems a valuable lesson on a day when card catalogues are dying, communications are deleted, and buildings crumble under the weight of society's expectations.

Danny sees Elijah's remorseful expression and doesn't know what to think. Does such an expression come from knowledge or innocence? Sometimes it's so hard to tell the difference.

The rain will not let up. For a moment, Elijah thinks he sees Julia, and his feelings zigzag. But it's not her – not her at all. She is no longer a person in his life; instead, she is a person that other people will remind him of.

Danny and Elijah run to a cafe, the dirt of Italy slowly gathering on their shoes and their legs. A bad case of the doldrums seems to have hit the natives along with the rain – the

243

waiters look glum, almost forlorn. Although Danny has picked up enough Italian to place his order, he is afraid that if he speaks a few words in Italian, the waiter will assume he knows more than a few words. So he sticks to English, thereby assuring that the waiter will not smile in return.

"So where do you want to go next?" Danny asks Elijah after the waiter has departed.

"I'd love to see the statue – you know, the one with the face that you can stick your hand in."

"The one from *Roman Holiday*?"

"Yes. Exactly. How did you know?"

Soon they are talking loudly, animatedly, impersonating Gregory Peck. They are reliving the movie and debating its finer points, agreeing only upon the ending.

How strange they must seem to the unimpressible Italian waiters and the pop-star Spanish teens and the Japanese image collectors and the umbrella-sticked British pensioners – two grown American brothers, talking about how Audrey Hepburn makes them cry.

Danny proposes a nap, and this time Elijah doesn't disagree. He is surprised when Danny stops at the door of the hotel.

"What the hell?" Danny shouts.

"What is it?" Elijah asks. Then he sees what Danny is seeing – a small swastika, drawn on the door of the d'Inghilterra. What's inexplicable is not just that it was put there, but that the hotel hasn't noticed – or has even kept it up.

Danny immediately pulls a pen from his pocket and begins to cross it out. Elijah keeps watch, but nobody stops them. The door is bleeding ink – Danny is pressing so hard that he is chipping off the paint.

"It's gone," Elijah tells him. And indeed it is – replaced by a dark, ugly blot.

Danny goes to complain to the manager, who appears sympathetic. Then the Silver brothers return to their room. Danny heads straight for the shower. Elijah writes belated postcards to his friends and waits his turn. He starts one postcard to Cal, then writes three more. Even though he'll see her tomorrow, he wants to give her something she will be able to keep. He tries not to think about Julia, and in the act of trying, he thinks about her. But she seems vague now. Not a part of the real story.

"All yours," Danny says when he gets out of the shower. He is wearing one of the hotel robes.

Elijah is gratified to find there's still hot water. He closes his eyes and breathes in the steam. When he looks down at the drain, he sees a small ring of hair. Danny's hair. It is irrefutable proof, but still Elijah asks himself, *Is Danny losing his hair?* This would mean that Danny is growing older. Is changing.

So strange.

Elijah's inner snapshot of Danny is long out of date. But he hasn't realised it until now.

"What are you looking at?" Danny asks when Elijah steps from the bathroom and stares at his hairline. (It looks fine. Although there is a little grey...)

"Nothing," Elijah says. "I can't believe we're this old."

"Tell me about it."

Danny is already under the covers. It is two in the afternoon. Sunlight filters through the window, but Elijah gets into his bed anyway.

"We'll walk around a little before dinner," Danny continues driftily. He is turned away from Elijah, but entirely conscious he is there. "You can tell me what you've been up to."

"OK." Elijah closes his eyes and imagines that afternoon is night.

"And then we'll have a nice dinner."

"Sounds good."

"And walk around some more."

"Sure."

"And then I'll teach you multiplication."

Elijah smiles. "Perfect."

"I'm glad that you're here."

"So am I. I'm sorry about – well, what happened."

"So am I."

Danny thinks this will be the end of the conversation, but then Elijah (thinking of Julia, thinking of Cal, thinking of college applications, thinking of the confusion and elation and mistakes of the past week) asks, "Is this what growing up is like?"

And Danny answers, "I think so."

They will stay together until they leave the next day.

ARRIVAL

After they get through customs (Elijah's pot having been left for the maid service in Rome), they are confronted by a throng of eager, peering faces. Danny scans the crowd and sees his parents a little way off. His mother is reading a magazine and his father is staring at the flight listing.

A little closer, Danny spots Elijah's friend – no doubt the one who dropped him off. This time, she's wearing a chauffeur's cap and jacket, the cap tilted at a Dietrich angle.

Elijah hasn't seen her yet.

"Hey, isn't that your girlfriend?" Danny asks.

Elijah takes a look and beams. Cal sees him and beams in return.

"She's not my girlfriend," he tells his brother.

"Well, maybe she should be," his brother advises.

Elijah doesn't know what to say to that. Because now Cal is jumping the queue, running over and giving him the most fabulous hug.

"Speak Italian to me!" she cries. "Welcome home!"

"What are you wearing?" Elijah asks gleefully.

"You will not believe how many seventy-year-old men I had to hit up before I could get me one of these. I should go return it. I'll be right back."

With that, she jets off again. Danny's gaze follows her – sure enough, she is handing the cap and jacket back to a shirt-sleeved older man.

Elijah keeps hearing Danny's words – Well, *maybe she should be*. He wonders if it could really be that simple. If something so obvious could actually be right.

"Elijah! Danny!" Their mother is calling them now. She, too, is beaming.

"C'mon," Danny says. Elijah picks up his bag and continues down the arrival pathway.

After the hellos, the thank-yous begin. The word "trickery" does not come up. Danny doesn't even think it any more.

When Mrs Silver asks her sons what their favourite part of the trip was, they overlap and finish each other's sentences.

"Oh, it had to be—"

"The Pantheon was the most incredible—"

"—thing I've—"

"—we've—"

"—ever seen. You wouldn't—"

"You wouldn't believe it."

Mrs Silver and Mr Silver share a knowing look.

Elijah and Danny continue on – the telling makes them realise what a good time they've had. Danny talks about gondoliers and Joseph and meeting Ari again, while Elijah tells them about the balcony over St Mark's Square, the floors and the ceilings, and the woman on the plane ride over who once met Billy Corgan. Julia is not mentioned – she is, momentarily, forgotten.

Mr Silver asks if all the hotels were OK. Mrs Silver asks if they had a chance to see the synagogues.

Elijah and Cal walk arm in arm as they all head to the garage.

The conversation falls back on to the usual post-vacation topics – what the weather was like here, what the weather was like there, what's been on the news. Cal clearly has other news to tell Elijah, but it will have to wait for the car ride home. Danny overhears her telling Elijah that Ivan and Meg had a falling-out in the middle of ballroom dance, and the implications are *huge*.

Finally, they reach the point where Cal's car is one direction and the Silvers' is the other.

Mr and Mrs Silver's desire to have Cal and Elijah over for dinner is overruled by their desire to have them drive home before sundown. Plus, Elijah has to be at work early the next day. ("Early" being ten o'clock.)

Elijah says thank you again and again. He hugs his mother and father... as does Cal. Then he comes over to Danny, and the two of them shake hands.

"Give me a break," Cal moans.

"Tell me about it," Mrs Silver puts in.

Elijah and Danny laugh and go for a hug. They hold on longer than either would have expected. When they let go, they thank each other and smile.

"Good luck."

"You too."

Then, with a wave, Cal and Elijah walk away.

Danny watches them go – arm in arm, fading into the garage.

As Elijah walks back into the land of the student, with its late-night coffee conversations and application anxieties, and as Danny returns to his voice-mail, e-mail, direct-deposit, pulse-driven existence, Danny wonders when he'll next see his brother. And what it will be like.

There is the distance of miles, and the distance of brothers, to overcome. He can feel the world coming between them again.

But the world is so much smaller than it used to be.

DAVID LEVITHAN

David Levithan è l'autore di *Boy Meets Boy* e *The Realm of Possibility*.
Attualmente egli vive nel New Jersey e viaggia spesso al di fuori
dei suoi confini. David non parla Italiano, e se voi non capite
questo paragrafo, anche voi non parlate Italiano.*

To find out more about him, check:
www.davidlevithan.com.

*David Levithan is the author of *Boy Meets Boy* and *The Realm of
Possibility*. He currently lives in New Jersey and travels outside of
it often. He does not speak Italian, and if you don't understand
this, you don't speak Italian, either.

Author of *Will Grayson, Will Grayson*
with John Green

BOY MEETS BOY

DAVID LEVITHAN

*Then he looks up at me. And then, after a beat, he breaks
out smiling. "Hey," he says, "I've been looking all over
for you." I don't know what to say. I am so happy
and so scared.*

Paul has been gay his whole life and he's confident
about almost everything. He doesn't have to hide
his feelings like best friend Tony or even cope with
loving the wrong guy like his other best friend Joni.

But heartbreak can happen to anyone. Falling in
love changes everything...

"Intimate, feel-good and quick-fire" *Guardian*
"Funny and clever and touching" *Telegraph*

Winner of the LAMDA Literary Award

OUT NOW

www.harpercollins.co.uk